Praise for
The Very, Very Far North

A *Booklist* Editors' Choice

★ "Wonderfully follow[s] in the tradition of A. A. Milne's
Winnie the Pooh stories. . . . Gentle humor, a personable
narrative voice, and some elevated vocabulary fortify the
simple, character-driven adventures, which will win over
young readers in a heartbeat."
—*Booklist*, starred review

"Quirky and imaginative—postmodern storytelling at its best."
—*Kirkus Reviews*

"Duane is kin to Winnie the Pooh, with an affable nature
and an endearing cluelessness that leads to moments of sage
wisdom. . . . Kiddos whose tastes tend toward the cozy will
find warmth and comfort in Duane's frosty world."
—*Bulletin of the Center for Children's Books*

"Each character is well developed and the kindness with
which these friends treat each other is instructive without
being didactic. . . . The rich language and wordplay make
for an excellent read-aloud."
—*School Library Journal*

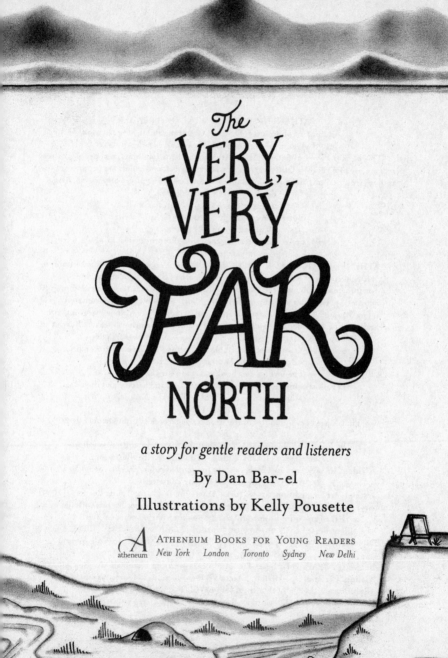

The VERY, VERY FAR NORTH

a story for gentle readers and listeners

By Dan Bar-el

Illustrations by Kelly Pousette

A
atheneum ATHENEUM BOOKS FOR YOUNG READERS

New York   London   Toronto   Sydney   New Delhi

ATHENEUM BOOKS FOR YOUNG READERS
An imprint of Simon & Schuster Children's Publishing Division
1230 Avenue of the Americas, New York, New York 10020

For information about special discounts for bulk purchases, please contact Simon & Schuster Special Sales at 1-866-506-1949 or business@simonandschuster.com.
The Simon & Schuster Speakers Bureau can bring authors to your live event. For more information or to book an event, contact the Simon & Schuster Speakers Bureau at 1-866-248-3049 or visit our website at www.simonspeakers.com.
Also available in an Atheneum Books for Young Readers hardcover edition
Book design by Lauren Rille and Karyn Lee
The text for this book was set in Mrs Eaves OT.
The illustrations for this book were rendered in charcoal and digital.
Manufactured in the United States of America
0522 MTN
First Atheneum Books for Young Readers paperback edition October 2020
4 6 8 10 9 7 5

The Library of Congress has cataloged the hardcover edition as follows:
Names: Bar-el, Dan, author. | Pousette, Kelly, illustrator.
Title: The very, very far north : a story for gentle readers and listeners / by Dan Bar-el ; illustrated by Kelly Pousette.
Description: First edition. | New York : Atheneum Books for Young Readers, [2019]
Summary: As Duane, a polar bear, explores his new home he makes friends with the wide variety of creatures he encounters, despite their varied personalities.
Identifiers: LCCN 2018037005 (print) | LCCN 2018042941 (eBook) | ISBN 9781534433434 (eBook) | ISBN 9781534433410 (hardcover : alk. paper) |ISBN 9781534433427 (paperback)
Subjects: | CYAC: Polar bear—Fiction. | Bears—Fiction. | Animals—Arctic regions—Fiction. | Friendship—Fiction. | Arctic regions—Fiction. | Humorous stories.
Classification: LCC PZ7.B250315 (eBook) | LCC PZ7.B250315 Ver 2019 (print) | DDC [Fic]—dc23 | LC record available at https://lccn.loc.gov/2018037005

For my father—a gentle man

—D. B.

For my own Dan, who I will forever adventure with

—K. P.

THE INTRODUCTION

I F YOU HEAD NORTH, really north, to the north part of north, where parallels and meridians tangle, where compasses get confused and chronometers lose confidence, and then once you reach *that* north, you go just a little bit farther north, that's where you'll find Duane and his friends.

It is a world apart, but it's familiar all the same.

Duane will likely greet you with the warm affection he shows for his friends

C.C., Magic, Handsome, and the others. He might offer you an icicle treat or ask your opinion on whether a mid-late-morning nap is preferable to a late-mid-afternoon nap. And if, during the first few minutes of your chat, you find yourself unable to stop staring, unable to overlook the fact that Duane is a polar bear, do not worry. Duane won't be upset. Duane rarely gets upset. He has only kindness in his heart, which is why his friends love him so.

But for those of you who have limited time, due to school or soccer practice, or because your parents need looking after, and making a long trek up north is just not possible at the moment, then the story I'm about to tell will tide you over until you are ready.

1.
DUANE ARRIVES, MAKES A FRIEND,
AND FINDS A HOME

AS THE STORY GOES, before there was Duane, there was C.C. Ask any of his friends, ask Sun Girl or Squint, and they would tell you the same.

One day, which is to say one Thursday, because all good stories start on a Thursday, Duane lumbered into the Very, Very Far North from somewhere else. It wasn't planned. It wasn't expected. But it was summertime, so in a drowsy, lackadaisical frame of mind, Duane followed the shoreline of the Cold, Cold Ocean, paying no attention to anything other than the sound of the gentle lapping water. Eventually, he found himself on a beach that slanted at just the right angle to make it ideal for napping. Even better, behind the beach were marshes filled with long, tasty grass, and set farther back were bushes and bushes of delicious wild berries.

Duane prized three activities above all others. Since two of them happened to be napping and eating, he found this place to be more than agreeable. In fact, right then a nap was insisting itself upon Duane, who yawned in complete agreement. But when Duane stretched himself on his back to warm his tummy in the summer sun at just the right angle, his eyes caught sight of something curious off the coast. It was a ship, or rather, it was a shipwreck. Duane was not well-informed enough to know what either a ship or a shipwreck was, but I can tell all of you who do know that the tall wooden ship that had run aground was old. Only one of the three masts remained unbroken, and none still held its sails. The hull listed to one side, and a very large, splintery gash marred the bow.

Duane studied the shipwreck with great interest because Duane was a polar bear in possession of a curious nature. In the right situation, a nap and a snack could sometimes be put off for a little exploring. Exploring was Duane's other most favorite activity. Toward the Cold, Cold Ocean he went, and with a splash, he was soon paddling to where his curiosity led.

He reached the shipwreck, swimming right through the gap, as the ship did not lack for seawater within, which sloshed back and forth against the thick wooden ribs of its dark belly.

Duane swam toward midship, where a set of steep stairs invited him up to a level still inside the ship but above the water's surface. With a couple of shakes, Duane dried himself off and began his exploring in earnest. Along the corridor were several rooms, some filled with boxes, others containing strange items he couldn't name, but sadly, none, as far as his nose could tell, had anything to do with food. At the very end of the passageway was a door, slightly ajar with light spilling out. Also spilling out was the sound of a well-spoken voice. The voice was speaking Latin, which you may know, but Duane did not, nor do I, so I'm afraid I cannot translate.

"*Cogito, cogitas, cogitat.*"

How curious, thought Duane, making his way closer. Written on the door with beautiful flourishes in gold paint was a name, but time had faded most of the letters away so all that remained were two capital *C*s. Duane, however, mistook them for two round eyes. When he pushed his snout through a gap, he was able to glimpse who was talking in that mysterious language.

"Ego descite, discis, et discit."

Perched upon a wide oak table, among more strange items, Duane spied a snowy owl reading from a large open book. I would hasten to add that she was a very serious-looking owl, but I'm not sure if owls come in any other variety.

"Hello," said Duane.

"*Rogo, rogas, rogat—*" The owl paused, looked up from the book, and rotated her head toward Duane. "Who might you be?" she inquired.

Here was a question never asked of Duane before. He gave it serious thought because he suspected that this was what the owl would want. "Well, I might be Kevin or Trevor . . . but I'd prefer to be myself, Duane."

"Duane the polar bear."

"Am I?" asked Duane.

"Most certainly," said the owl with a curt nod. "I can show you a drawing of a creature that quite resembles you, and beneath the drawing it states emphatically that you are a polar bear."

Using her wing, the owl flipped quickly through many pages of the book that sat on the table in front of her until she stopped and pointed with her other wing. Duane ventured closer and looked over the owl's shoulder. "Huh! So I am."

"And will you, Duane the polar bear, be staying here?"

"Here?" Duane looked around the room, with its many bookshelves and metal objects and such. Everything looked hard and had sharp edges. Other than the back wall, which consisted of mainly windows that allowed in lots of light, it was not nap-friendly in the least. And besides, wouldn't it be an imposition? Duane felt he wasn't anything more than an uninvited guest or a well-intentioned intruder. "Isn't this *your* home?"

"It wasn't at first, but it is now. I've grown fond of the library and the scientific instruments."

"I'm not sure that I'd be comfortable here myself."

"According to this book, you prefer living in snow caves."

"According to me, as well," agreed Duane, who considered himself more and more of an expert on the subject.

"However, we're currently short of snow, it being summer. If you are willing to adapt, there is a rock cave not far from the beach you were about to take a nap upon. Follow me and I'll show you."

The owl took off from the table, flew out of one of the open windows, and then upward out of sight. Two polar-bear blinks later, she returned to find Duane standing exactly where she left him. "I should have mentioned that there is a set of stairs at the far end of the corridor that leads above deck."

"Ah," said Duane in understanding.

When they reunited atop the broken ship,

Duane had thought up a question. "How did you know I was going to nap on the beach?"

"I used this telescope," she said, flying over to the ship's bow and perching upon a long brass tube mounted on a tripod. "Come look through this end."

Duane did, and sure enough, there was the beach and the delicious grass and berry bushes, as if they were close enough to nibble on. But when the owl tilted the opposite end of the telescope up a bit, Duane could see a rock cave built into a hillside behind a field.

"It's a very large cave," explained the owl,

"big enough for a polar bear's needs, and not presently occupied."

Duane had come from somewhere else, and now he was here. But what was here? Here was an excellent cave, and here was a perfect beach, and here was a place with plenty to eat. More importantly, even to a polar bear that puts napping and eating high on his priority list, here was a snowy owl nearby. She seemed very smart. She seemed very helpful. She seemed as if she could be a friend.

"I'll take it," said Duane, resolute. "Thank you, See-See."

The owl now seemed surprised and puzzled. She flew off the telescope and landed a few feet away upon the unbroken mast. "Why did you call me C.C.?"

"It was on the door of your room. Two big round eyes to see with. I assumed it was your name." What Duane did not know, but which I will tell you right now, is that before that moment, the owl had never been called See-See or C.C. It is still unclear whether the owl had any name at all prior to the one Duane gave her. Duane would eventually give names to all of his friends except for one, but C.C., as I shall now spell it, was his first. "Is it not your name?"

"It wasn't, but on consideration, I think it shall be," replied C.C. with another curt nod. "You're very good at giving names, Duane the polar bear."

This made Duane very happy, not just because he discovered a new talent, but also because giving a compliment is what friends do, and C.C. had done just that.

So Duane swam back from the shipwreck to claim his new home. He discovered that inside the cave was a soft feather mattress, somewhat old and musty, but still bliss to lie upon. Duane was enthralled.

Before he tucked in for the night, Duane stood silently at the mouth of his cave to take in the lovely view. In the far distance, he saw the Cold, Cold Ocean and the shipwreck. At a closer distance, the Fabulous Beach, as he would now call it, and closer still, the marshes and the berry bushes. In the field just below him, to his surprise, he spotted a musk ox. The musk ox was standing beside a pond, staring lovingly at his own reflection. Whether that musk ox had a name prior to when Duane came along is also up for debate, but for now, let us end this story with Duane drifting off to sleep on his soft feather mattress, wondering about that musk ox and hoping that they too might eventually become friends.

2.
DUANE MAKES HIS HOME HOMIER AND GETS TO KNOW HIS NEIGHBOR

IN THE WEEKS THAT followed Duane's arrival to the Very, Very Far North, he set for himself the goal of making his new cave as cozy as it could be. It was the mattress left behind by whomever had lived there earlier that had inspired him. Such softness was a new and wonderful experience for Duane. He could hardly believe that a nap could be made even more pleasant than it already was, but the mattress definitely proved so, and it led him to consider what other items might bring unexpected delight into his life.

C.C. suggested that the mattress was most likely brought over from the Shipwreck, as Duane now called the place where she lived. She said, "As long as you would be kind enough not to remove the books and scientific objects from my room, I don't see any reason why you can't borrow anything else onboard."

So Duane rummaged from room to room, putting together items he would like to bring back to his cave. A table, some chairs, a set of drawers to keep any interesting things he might find on an adventure—these were the first pieces Duane chose to take. Also at C.C.'s suggestion, Duane used a small boat that was tied to the Shipwreck to carry everything back to shore. He named the small boat the Wreck-*less* on account of it not suffering a big hole that would cause it to sink.

Back and forth, Duane swam from the Shipwreck to the beach, pulling the Wreck-*less* by a
rope that he held between his teeth. It was hard
work, both the swimming and later, the carrying, because then he had to bring the objects
from the beach up to his much higher cave.
Harder still were the unexpected interruptions
whenever he passed the field where his neighbor, the musk ox, made his home.

The friendship that Duane had so hoped
would blossom between the two of them had
not yet progressed beyond occasional hellos.
The musk ox was often too preoccupied
with . . . well, himself, and his reflection
in the large pond. But this day was different. Breaking his gaze, the musk ox would
ask Duane the same question, each and every
time Duane walked by.

"And what have you there?" the musk ox

would say, despite it being fairly obvious what was in Duane's arms.

On the first trip to his cave, Duane was carrying a table. Without putting it down, Duane stopped and replied, "It's a table."

"Yes, yes, so I see, so I see," commented the musk ox, returning to his reflection.

Assuming the conversation was finished, Duane continued up the hill toward his cave when he was addressed by the musk ox a second time. "For what will you be using it?"

Still holding the table, which was feeling increasingly heavier, Duane turned around to respond. "Oh, I don't know. I thought that it would be nice to eat breakfast at or to keep a

vase of wildflowers on, to cheer the cave up."

"Yes, yes, that would be proper," agreed the musk ox.

Duane watched him return his attention once more to the pond before twisting his heavy load back in the direction of the cave. He could feel his front paws weakening with the effort of holding the table while he climbed.

"*Do* you have a vase?"

Duane stopped momentarily and let out 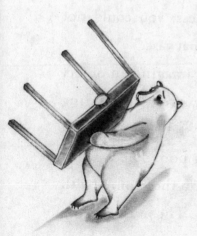 a brief whimper. Taking a deep breath, he gathered his waning strength in order to turn and politely face his neighbor. Duane then bent backward so that some of the table's weight rested on his belly, which was uncomfortable but did help prevent gravity from taking both him and the table forward and back down the hill at a speed faster than deemed safe. "Do I have a what?" he struggled to ask.

None of Duane's efforts of endurance seemed to interest the musk ox in the least. "I was simply inquiring whether you were in possession of a vase for the wildflowers of which you spoke. My great-aunt once had a spectacular vase. I shall never forget it. Painted in the lightest of blues, with twisting vinelike handles, one could only admire its daintiness. But heavy? My goodness, you could not imagine an object as heavy as that vase."

In fact, Duane could well imagine an object so heavy because he was currently buckling under the weight of the heavy table. Lower and lower his back arched as his poor knees bent, eventually bringing him flat on the ground with the table straddled above him. The musk ox gave

Duane a disapproving look. "You don't intend on leaving the table there, I trust."

"Just for a minute or two," said Duane in a faint voice.

On subsequent trips, when he passed by the field and the musk ox inquired of what was in his arms, Duane would put down the chairs or dresser or box of knickknacks and not lift them again until he was absolutely sure that the musk ox had asked every possible question and related every memory that came up within the conversation. In that way, Duane managed to complete his journeys without collapsing from sheer exhaustion.

Late in the day, Duane returned the *Wreckless*, believing he had completed transforming his cave into a cozy home. He intended on popping in to say goodbye to C.C., who had been very helpful, but instead, on a whim, he had one last rummage. Making his way deeper into a large, shadowy room filled from floor to ceiling with this and that, Duane spotted something as tall as he, but thinner, with a very round face and no hands or arms. He rushed to find C.C.

"What's that?" Duane asked her, once back in the room.

"My book tells me that it's a grandfather clock," explained C.C. "I am currently in possession of what is called a pocket watch, which is similar in purpose but a great deal smaller."

"Will it grow up into a grandfather clock?" Duane wondered.

"I have asked that very same question. My current hypothesis is that it will, but ultimately, it will be a wait-and-see situation."

"You said it has a purpose. What purpose does it have?"

"To tell you the time," replied C.C.

Duane found that a curious thought. "But isn't the time always now?"

The smart and well-read owl hesitated. "*Ahem*, yes, I suppose . . . but when *is* now? Is now the morning, or is it noon, or is it late at night? Do you see the complications?"

Duane did not. "I know it isn't morning because I already ate breakfast. I had berries. They were delicious. I know it isn't noon because I already felt the sun losing interest in the day and heading off to wherever it goes. I put 'now' sometime between late afternoon and evening because if it were night, I probably couldn't see you."

The deep-thinking owl stared at the polar bear for a good long time, unable to come up with a countering argument, so she changed the subject instead. "Time has not been good to this grandfather clock. The hands on its face have fallen off, making it impossible to tell if it's four twenty-eight, or eight forty-two, or seven thirty, or a quarter to nine."

Duane understood nothing that C.C. had just said other than that it used to have hands on its face, which, in the way that Duane understood it to mean, was really more of a *misunder-standing* than an understanding. *Hands on its face?* he wondered.

"This grandfather clock has lost its purpose," C.C. continued.

Duane found that terribly sad news. He came closer to the grandfather clock, with a strong desire to console it. Then he thought he heard something. Duane put his ear up against the side of the clock and listened closely. "It sounds like large water drops falling from a melting icicle and hitting a puddle. Is the poor old thing melting, too?"

"Your observation skills are admirable, Duane the polar bear, but your conjecturing needs work. It's not melting; it's tocking."

"Really? Is it talking to me?" he asked, completely misunderstanding again. Duane addressed the object in an apologetic tone. "I'm afraid I don't speak Clock."

"No, Duane, I meant it was *tick*-tocking. That's what clocks and watches do." Using her beak, C.C. pried open a long thin door in the belly of the clock, thus revealing an intricate display of rusted gears and springs and chains and doodads creaking away. "A clock is a machine."

"That tells what time now is," Duane stated with growing confidence.

"Yes. When it works correctly. When it has its hands," C.C. clarified.

"Which this one doesn't," Duane said sympathetically.

"No," agreed C.C. "This grandfather clock will tick-tock away, but to no end, to no purpose."

The owl and the polar bear stood silently, as if to pay respect to the clock's woeful, abandoned state. It was a solemn, heavy moment until Duane's expression suddenly brightened with a big smile. "Perfect! I'll take it!" he said, lifting the grandfather clock up in a bear hug.

"B-b-but why?" sputtered C.C. "It won't tell you anything."

"No," agreed the polar bear, "but it will suggest possibilities, and that's always exciting." Then Duane, concerned that the time was late because he could see the blackening sky, and wanting to avoid climbing up to his cave with the heavy clock in complete darkness, began lugging it to the Wreck-*less*.

C.C. was an owl who preferred sensible

answers, and Duane's answer was not nearly close enough to meeting her standard. "What possibilities?" she demanded while in pursuit.

"Well, maybe, at a certain time in the future, I will come across a delicious chocolate cake."

"Yes, perhaps," agreed C.C. "But the grand-father clock can't tell you when that might happen."

"And it can't tell me when that might *not* happen either, on account of its having no hands. So it remains a possibility." Duane loaded the clock onto the boat and took hold of the rope. "Good night, C.C. I'll return the Wreck-*less* tomorrow." With a small splash, he was in the water, pulling his clock toward the shore.

He left the snowy owl standing onboard the Shipwreck in a confused state, with eyes slightly wider than they naturally were. "It's not a matter of when. It's a matter of if!" she finally shouted. "Did you hear me? Duane?" Perhaps he heard her or perhaps not, but either way, he had the rope between his teeth, so a reply would have been difficult.

That night, Duane lay upon his so-soft mattress, looking over his table and chairs, his dresser and his assorted knickknacks. When he had awoken that morning, he had next to nothing in his cave, but now he had a cozy home. At the other side of his cave stood the grandfather clock tocking away. Duane was starting to understand how clocks speak and what they were saying. Clocks were not so much interested in now but later, in the future. For example, ten minutes from now, or twenty or ninety, a rainfall may begin. Or not. In an hour Duane might hear the musk ox loudly snoring from his field below. Or not. The only thing you knew for sure was that something was going to happen, which made things exciting. On that, the grandfather clock and Duane agreed.

3.
THE MUSK OX IS GIVEN HIS NAME, AND AN ADVENTURE BEGINS

There was an itch in Duane's feet when he awoke one fine cold morning at the beginning of autumn. It wasn't a scratchy itch that could be relieved with a paw. It wasn't a *rashy* itch that required C.C.'s medical opinion. No, this was a curiosity itch, which meant that it was a day for exploring, no two ways about it. So after a breakfast bowl of berries, Duane was out of his cave, following where his curiosity led.

"Good morning," Duane said to his closest neighbor, the musk ox.

The musk ox was deeply engrossed in his reflection in the pond, turning his head to one side and then the other. Since making his acquaintance, Duane had soon realized that spending hours studying himself was the musk ox's favorite activity.

"Hmm? Oh, hello, Duane."

Like the polar bear, the musk ox had come into the Very, Very Far North from somewhere

else, and he had chosen the large open field as his home. The pond within the field, with its amazingly clear reflective abilities, made a big impression. However, as the days grew colder, in the mornings ice was starting to form on the pond's surface, which later cracked and distorted the view. The musk ox was not happy about this.

"I'm off to do a little exploring," Duane announced. "I'm going to cross the river below the Rocky Ridge and see what there is to see. Would you care to join me?"

The musk ox spoke in a low voice, stretching his words out from time to time. There are those who would say he sounded snobbish or haughty or self-important. I will leave it to you to form your own opinion. "Will this be a social excursion, Duane? Will we be hobnobbing?"

Duane sometimes had difficulty understanding the musk ox, who once explained that his formal education gave him an expansive vocabulary. Duane did not understand that part either. But the musk ox was never offended. He simply found other words to say what he wanted to say.

"Will we be meeting others?"

"Oh, I see." Duane nodded. "I don't know if we will. That's the best part of exploring. You never know what may happen."

From the musk ox's expression, one might conclude that not knowing what may happen was the *worst* part of exploring. "I am currently not presentable for public viewing. I will accompany you to the river, but no farther."

This was a compromise, and Duane was good at compromises. "Wonderful," he said. "I will enjoy your company for as long as you can give it."

But would he enjoy it? Over the past few weeks, Duane had discovered that the musk ox had few interests, and of those few, his top interest was by far himself. He loved to talk about himself, although often there was a hum of worry within his words. To prove this point, I need only to recount the first thing that came out of his mouth as he left his field with Duane. "These cold mornings are freezing up the pond and playing havoc with my reflection. The ice cracks and distorts it. I couldn't tell if I was looking at something hideous or handsome. I do have my doubts when I cannot see myself."

Duane had no reply. Although he reflected upon what he saw around him, Duane rarely looked at his own reflection. It wasn't a concern. Duane never had doubts just because he couldn't see himself. *I am a polar bear, so I likely have polar bear features*, he thought. And just by thinking that thought, it gave him another thought. *I think, therefore I am a polar bear.*

The musk ox mistook Duane's silence for indifference. "You just don't understand, Duane," he said gloomily.

Duane nodded. He didn't understand. Not really. There was so much he didn't understand. But he felt that the musk ox needed some cheer, so he took a chance. "You're always handsome," Duane said reassuringly.

"Yes, that is kind of you, but—"

"Also," Duane continued on boldly, "*I* think that since I have a name you can call *me*, which is Duane, then it is only fair that there be a name that I can call *you*."

"Oh?" said the musk ox, taken aback by Duane's unusually forceful voice. "What, er, what did you have in mind?"

Duane smiled. "Why, Handsome, of course.

May I call you Handsome? It would make things so much easier."

If the musk ox were telling this story, he would tell you that Duane's suggestion left him gobsmacked, and that likely would have left you scratching your head like Duane and wondering what "gobsmacked" meant. It meant that the musk ox was stunned and speechless . . . for a few seconds anyway, until he found his voice again.

"Handsome. I would be referred to *as* Handsome?"

"Yes," said Duane, "if that's all right."

The musk ox swallowed what appeared to be a large lump in this throat. "Yes, that would be acceptable." And so from this point forward, I too will call the musk ox Handsome.

Duane and Handsome continued their trek in a much lighter mood, which suited Duane just fine. Paying attention to what is around you is really what exploring is all about. The minute you start worrying about whether you cleaned your breakfast bowl before you left your cave, you've missed something interesting right in front of your face. *Light mood, positive spirit, bouncy steps*, thought Duane. *These are the ideal things to bring along when exploring.*

Eventually they reached the Rocky Ridge that ran the length of the river. Looking down upon the water, Duane took notice of its great width. He imagined how excellent it would be for sliding across on his belly when winter came and the surface froze. But for now, he wondered if this was where he would part company with Handsome or whether he could coax the musk ox into continuing on as one half of their exploring team.

"Would you care to join me for a swim across to the other side?" Duane asked hopefully.

"We've done so well exploring already."

Handsome looked upon the river with something less than enthusiasm. "My family has never been big on aquatic sports. All that splashing about and watery muck getting caught in one's fur . . ."

"Oh, I see," said Duane with a touch of sadness.

Sensing Duane's disappointment, and genuinely wanting to show some gratitude for his new name, Handsome added, "Otherwise, I'd be more than willing to continue on."

Duane lifted his eyes. "You would?"

"Oh, yes," Handsome declared, now getting carried away with his show of gratitude. "If not for the water, I would be with you each step of the way on this adventure." Handsome realized how easy it was to make big generous pledges when he was not obliged to live up to them, so he went on. "I would climb mountains and tra-verse dangerous cliff paths. I would poke my head into dark caves and push over heavy boul-ders."

That cheered up Duane considerably. "You really would do that?"

"Without a second thought," Handsome declared. "In the name of exploration, I would do all those things and much more . . . were it not for the bit involving swimming."

Such good news, Duane thought. "Well, in that case, let's forget about swimming and instead continue exploring farther up to see if there is another way to get across."

Handsome's heroic face suddenly slumped. "Pardon me?"

"I had no idea that you were so passionate about exploring, Handsome. I suggest we go exploring for a very long time. To be honest, when we left this morning, I was hoping to be home for lunch, but now, after hearing you talk, I'd even be willing to skip lunch to explore some more."

Handsome swallowed another lump in his throat before speaking. "You would?"

"Absolutely." Duane nodded.

"But you adore lunch, as do I. It's one of the things we have in common."

"Along with exploring, so it would seem." Duane smiled. "Isn't this excellent?"

"Hmm," replied Handsome.

With renewed determination, at least on Duane's part, the two explorers followed the river upstream in the hope of finding a less splashy way across it. To Duane's delight, there was a definite narrowing of its width, but to Handsome's regret, the ground was climbing higher and higher as well.

"It's getting steeper, wouldn't you say?" asked Duane, excited at this new challenge.

"I, *huff, huff*, would, *huff, huff*, say so," gasped Handsome, "if I *huff, huff*, could only, *huff, huff*, catch, *huff, huff*, my breath."

"This way!" shouted Duane, far in the lead. "I hear something thundering and roaring above us! It could be a monster! Wouldn't *that* be exciting?"

"Hmm," growled Handsome.

The steep, rocky terrain forced them to leave the river and approach the loud noise from the side. After Duane plotted a route that Handsome would be able to manage, he stepped around a jagged corner, and there before him was not a monster but a tall, thin waterfall. The water crashed down from a stone lip high above. Mist rose from the pool below it, and the sunlight that pierced it created a double rainbow.

"You don't see that every day, do you?" said Duane, marveling at the sight.

Handsome marveled too, but from a farther distance, leaning against a large rock while his tired legs steadied.

Duane was most pleased with how the exploring was going. Later, when he would tell C.C. about the great adventure, she would explain that the reason for the success was because it was a Thursday. "Scientifically speaking, Duane," she would say, "all good things happen on a Thursday. It's just basic physics."

Handsome might have had a different hypothesis about Thursdays. He was exhausted and hungry and sweaty. He could only imagine how unpresentable he looked, but he purposely didn't imagine it because the embarrassment would be too great. Enough was enough. The exploring would have to come to a close. A musk ox of his refinement cannot spend the day traipsing up and down, getting his fur all sweaty and unmanageable. Handsome cleared his throat. A stern speech was in order. "Duane, I must put my hoof down in no uncertain terms and insist that we return back to—"

The polar bear was no longer there.

"Duane?" asked Handsome, confused.

The polar bear was not elsewhere, either.

"Duane?" asked Handsome, concerned.

The polar bear was no longer anywhere.

"Duane!" Handsome shouted, fearing the worst.

"I'm up here!" Duane shouted back.

Handsome looked up and saw Duane standing high above, beside the waterfall, waving enthusiastically. "Hurry, Handsome! I have something wonderful to show you! If you were excited about exploring before, you will be even

more excited once
you climb up here!"
The musk ox
stood silently beside
the double rainbow.
He had a slight twitch
in his left eye. He looked
up again at Duane, who was
still cheerfully waving. Handsome tried to smile
back, but his heart simply wasn't in it. Instead,
he mumbled something under his breath about
creating a law to ban all exploring in his neigh-
borhood, before sighing and finally heading up
to join Duane.

4.
THE ADVENTURE CONTINUES UNTIL
HANDSOME HAS HAD ENOUGH

WE ENDED THE LAST story with Duane in a
very good mood, standing at the top of the
waterfall, and Handsome in a very dark mood,
grumbling at the bottom.

Duane was happy because
he had discovered two
things that would allow
them to continue on
with their exploration.

For one, the river appeared to be at its narrowest. For another, Duane counted a half dozen large rocks with flat tops sticking out of the river, spaced close enough for a polar bear or musk ox to make his way to the other side and not get wet.

Handsome was unhappy because he had discovered that you should not make boasts about how much you love exploring and hiking and climbing if the truth is you absolutely don't.

So while Handsome unhappily trudged up the steep hill to join Duane, I will take this opportunity to inform you that there was someone on the other side of the river, hidden from view behind a hillock. That someone in question was Major Puff, who is a puffin, and if you've never met a puffin before, I will explain that it is a short black-and-white bird with a rounded chest and a large beak, which is orange and gray in color. You may think that what I've described is a very pleasant-looking bird. You may also think that a pleasant-looking bird would have an agreeable nature, and that may be true. However, this particular puffin, Major Puff, doesn't always make the best first impression, which is why I thought I'd step in now.

Major Puff will tell you that he comes from a long line of military heroes. He will tell you this often and in great detail, whether you want to hear it or not. Major Puff knows all about the glorious battles of the past, most involving the puffins' wicked and vile enemy, the great black-backed gulls. For hundreds of years, these vicious foes have fought dirty. They've attempted to bring disorder and destruction upon the puffin nation. And for centuries too, Major Puff's ancestors have led the way to victory each and every time. Major Puff is very proud of his lineage. It means that he is a puffin of good breeding, possessing the qualities of honor and bravery.

Also worth mentioning is that Major Puff has not been in battle himself. He has not been tested, so to speak. Nor has he ever seen a great black-backed gull face to face, which keeps him on continuous guard should he find himself in close proximity with his archenemy without knowing it.

But what Major Puff does very well is march. He is extraordinarily good at marching because he practices every day. Back straight, chest out, chin at a ninety-degree angle, he marches with

stiff legs, advancing for hours on end. And so we find Major Puff, marching back and forth, back and forth, behind a hillock and out of sight of Duane and Handsome, who will soon cross the river. Among the benefits of marching is, of course, battle preparedness, as well as physical fitness, but it also helps a puffin think, and Major Puff had something important to think about at that moment.

As the last hints of summer faded, Major Puff was deep in deliberation on whether or not to migrate south. Major Puff didn't really *have* to migrate south for winter. There was no instinct compelling him or any puffin to fly south. But

Major Puff liked the idea of going somewhere warm for a few months each year, or every other year, or whenever the mood struck him. Yet he didn't want to call it a holiday. Holidays were frivolous and silly, whereas a migration sounded much more serious and responsible, befitting a puffin of the military class. Migrations were traditional, as well, and Major Puff was all for keeping up traditions. Decision made!

On the other hand . . .

Maybe he should spend the winter staying put in the Very, Very Far North. Remaining there would have nothing to do with his overwhelming fear about flying in general or the great danger and difficulty of a migration in particular. Oh, no. It's more likely that he just found winter a delight. And it would be a shame to leave, missing out on all that freezing cold wintry splendor. Oh, and his staying would

also not have anything do with him not wanting to leave the burrow-home that he heroically
captured last spring, once he was sure no one
else was living there anymore. Major Puff always
heroically captured empty burrow-homes. It
was the puffin way.

Back and forth, back and forth, left, right,
left, right . . . a decision was not soon coming.
So let us return now to the other side of the
river at the moment when Handsome reached
Duane.

"Duane, *huff, huff,* I must tell you, *huff, huff,*
that I can't possibly, *huff, huff,* continue, *huff, huff,*
on this explo—"

"Look, Handsome!" Duane interrupted. "A
river crossing made of rocks! How fortunate.
And look behind us. That's my cave, and there is
your field, ever so close. We didn't even need to
climb up this very steep hill. Isn't that funny?"

"Hmm," said Handsome without a trace of amusement. Sweat dripped from his fur.

"Since it was your spirit of exploration that brought us here, Handsome, it seems only fitting that you should cross the river first." Duane respectfully stepped aside, allowing room for the musk ox to take the lead.

"But I couldn't," said Handsome politely but nervously.

"But I insist," said Duane with a humble nod.

Handsome studied the rocks with intense mistrust. He stretched one of his front hooves onto the closest rock, testing it for any wobbliness. It held firm. He looked over at Duane, who was still smiling and giving him encouraging tilts of his head toward the river.

"Hmm," Handsome said again, this time without a trace of eagerness, and then resigning himself to the task, he stepped up onto the first rock, which did not wobble, although Handsome did plenty of wobbling for the both of them. "Oh my! This is not comfortable! I am not steady, Duane. I am not steady!"

"You're doing great," Duane responded. "But keep going so not all your hooves are on the same rock."

With front legs shaking, Handsome forced himself to take another step so that now he straddled two rocks, with his belly hanging over the water that rushed between them. At first, his balance steadied, but then, because Handsome was staring down at the moving river, it brought on a spell of dizziness that caused him to sway this way and that. "Oh my! This is not comfortable in the least! I am not steady, Duane. I am not steady!"

Handsome's shouts of distress pulled Major

Puff out of his deep pondering about migration. His training threw him into immediate action. He marched up to the top of the hillock to learn what the commotion was about.

"What's all this, then?" he wondered aloud.

Spying down from his high perch, Major Puff saw two creatures he'd never met before. Both of them were much larger than he. One was on the far side of the river, covered in white fur, but it was the other one, standing on two rocks in the middle of the river, covered in long strands of black hair, that gave Major Puff pause.

"Could it be?" he asked himself, his eyes narrowing. "Could it be that I have come face to face with my mortal enemy, the great black-backed gull?"

Of course, he hadn't, because the great black-backed gull was a bird, and although it was a bigger bird than a puffin, it was not nearly as big as a musk ox. But good luck telling the Major at that moment. For Major Puff, this was the hour of reckoning. All those years of marching would finally pay off. Was he afraid? Of course he was afraid. But what soldier isn't afraid when he goes into battle?

"Get ahold of yourself," Major Puff ordered when his feet refused to march and his wings refused to flap. "Certainly the great black-backed gull is much larger than I imagined from the stories I was told. And most certainly no one ever mentioned those menacing horns on its head, or the four muscular legs. But you're a Puff! From a long line of Puffs! And no Puff has ever refused the call to battle."

This inspiring speech did the trick. Major Puff thrust out his chest defiantly and proceeded to march down the hillock toward his enemy.

As for Handsome, had he been a great black-backed gull, he would have likely flown back to the comfort of his field and reflection pond by now. But that not being the case, he was stuck in the middle of the river, feeling very miserable and very anxious. Handsome paid zero attention to the small puffin marching heroically toward him because his concerns lay elsewhere.

"I cannot do this, Duane," he cried from atop the two river rocks.

"You can, Handsome. Just a few more steps and you'll be on the other side where the real exploring can take place."

"But I don't like exploring!"

"Oh?" asked Duane, surprised. "You said that you loved exploring."

Handsome sighed and looked over his shoulder at Duane. When he finally spoke, his voice croaked with misery. "I exaggerated. Or maybe I lied. I can't tell the difference. Is there a difference? No matter. Duane, there is peril in this journey. I am not an admirer of peril. All this danger is causing worry lines on my face. I will be scarred for life! No sooner am I given the name Handsome, befitting my appearance, than my circumstances turn me hideous. I am tired and sweaty and disheveled. I want to go home."

This was a lot of information for Duane to take in. His partner was not as eager as he had hoped or thought. Duane wondered if in some way he was responsible for pushing Handsome on this adventure. He wondered if he hadn't listened carefully to Handsome. Duane wanted company, but perhaps this wasn't the sort of activity best suited for Handsome's company. Friendship is hard work, Duane realized. In the meantime, his friend truly did need help.

"Handsome, it would be much easier for you to go forward and turn around on the other side than for you to back up, wouldn't you agree?"

Handsome sniffed away his tears and gathered his thoughts. For a large musk ox, turning around in the middle of the river would be as impossible as blindly stepping backward, as Duane had pointed out. Sadly, it seemed that going across in order to come back was the best alternative. "Very well," he said weakly. "One must do what one must do."

The musk ox turned his head toward the far bank, determined to take the necessary steps.

"Halt! None shall pass!" shouted a short black-and-white creature with an orange-and-gray beak, standing at the river's edge.

"What? Oh, you've got to be kidding me!" said Handsome. He so desperately wanted this ordeal to be over with.

"Do not test my mettle, dastardly villain!" warned Major Puff.

"Dastardly villain? Look, whoever you are, I just want to get across so I can go back again. If you would be so kind as to clear a path . . ."

Major Puff scoffed at the suggestion and then boldly hopped forward several times so that he stood upon a river rock directly in front of Handsome. This took Handsome completely by surprise, causing him to lose his balance again. "Do great black-backed gulls think puffins are so foolish as to fall for *that* trick?" Major Puff shouted up at the musk ox.

"Great-backed what? Puffins? What on earth are you babbling on about? Let me pass!"

"Never!" Major Puff flapped his wings dramatically, causing Handsome to flinch and nearly fall over.

"Stop that! It's very annoying!"

"Ha!" Major Puff was quite caught up in his campaign. Puffin history was being made in this glorious moment. How they would sing praises of his valiant stand against what must assuredly be the largest great black-backed gull ever encountered! Major Puff the Ironhearted, they would call him. Major Puff the Wall of Strength. Major Puff the—

"Excuse me?" said a voice.

Jolted out of his daydream, Major Puff leaned his head to the right in order to peer around the thick legs of the musk ox. Also leaning to the side, in order to peer back at the puffin, was a polar bear.

"Excuse me," Duane said again, "but I don't believe we've met. My name is Duane."

The puffin scowled. "Major Puff has no interest in meeting the friend of my enemy."

"Oh," said Duane, taking note that this stranger already had a name. "So you two have met before, Major Puff?"

The puffin opened his mouth to speak but hesitated. ". . . Ah, no . . . not exactly."

"Then how do you know that you're enemies?"

Major Puff was outraged. "Are you suggesting that I might be friends with this fiend? He and all other great black-backed gulls are a scourge! A curse and a menace to all puffins! They steal and fight without honor. They are the lowest of the low!"

"I'm standing right here!" exclaimed Handsome, who was still caught in the middle of the river. "And as much as your name-calling stings my heart, it would sting so much more if I was, in fact, a great black-backed gull and NOT a musk ox!"

"A likely story," spat the puffin. "How you great black-backed gulls love to lie."

Handsome reached his patience's limit, and through his frustration with Major Puff, he found the resolve to fix his situation. "I've had enough. I'm coming across. You, sir, have been warned."

Handsome was readying himself to step onto the rock where Major Puff presently stood when suddenly the puffin boldly shouted, "Finally, a real battle! Take that!" while hopping backward away from Handsome.

This confused Handsome, since it sounded as if he were under attack, while at the same time, the puffin had actually cleared space for him to move. Handsome stepped forward to the next rock.

"Take that!" Major Puff shouted again while hopping back another step. "And that, and that!" he added, taking two more steps back.

"Take what? All you are doing is running away."

"Aha! So you've had enough, have you?" declared Major Puff victoriously from an even farther distance.

Worth noting at this point is that the most

important military tactic for puffins is the retreat. A puffin marches into battle in order to heroically run away, or fly away, but in either case, it's the "away" part that's crucial. In the telling of any great puffin battle, there reaches a point when the puffin fearlessly avoids pain and injury by courageously keeping out of reach of their enemies.

"I will accept nothing less than your total surrender," said Major Puff.

The puffin and the musk ox were now on the opposite side of the river from Duane. "So you're saying that unless I surrender, you will continue to move away from me?" Handsome asked.

"Those are my terms," said the puffin sternly.

Handsome turned his head toward Duane with an expression of complete bewilderment.

5.
DUANE AND C·C· REACH AN UNDERSTANDING

IN THE WEEKS THAT followed, the coldest season—that is to say, the best season—arrived in the Very, Very Far North. The temperature dropped and the snow fell. And it fell. And it fell. And it fell. The Cold, Cold Ocean turned into the Mainly Frozen Ocean. The sharp edges of the world softened under the crystal white, crunchy white, at times blinding white, and at other times muted white of the long, long months of winter.

Icicles now hung from the mouth of Duane's cave. Handsome's reflection pond stayed darkly ice-covered from morning to night. And in order to visit C.C. at the Shipwreck, one only had to stroll across the solid surface of the Mainly Frozen Ocean; swimming was no longer required.

To say that Duane liked the ice and snow was putting it mildly. He loved walking on snow; he loved sliding on ice. He loved tasting snow cakes, and he loved licking icicle pops. He loved lying in the snow and playing in the snow and sitting in the snow while staring at ice shapes in all their sculptural beauty. There might be many things that Duane could do without in the world, but snow and ice were not among them.

The nights were longer in the winter season, and that suited Duane as well, because it meant nap times could go on for longer. As a polar bear, Duane was not obligated to hibernate. Hibernation would be too much sleeping, even by Duane's standards. Hibernation would mean missing out on winter altogether and not having the opportunity to partake of all the things he loved about it. Still, as winter unfolded, his naps did tend to increase, stretching from hours at a time to days at a time. By winter's end, he could spend several weeks at a stretch asleep in his cave. Was he lazy? Perhaps. Duane didn't feel lazy. His long naps seemed in tune with the Very, Very Far North's yawning quiet, as if the world was already napping and he was just joining in.

But this story takes place in the early days of winter, when Duane's naps were long, but not too long. He had awoken late in the morning to a sunny day that painted the snowy landscape in dazzling ivory hues. Duane sauntered over to the mouth of his cave and snapped off a hanging icicle for breakfast. Then, without a second thought, and without even a plan, he continued walking out of his home, still groggy, licking his icicle pop, looking about but not really looking, just feeling the warm sunshine on his nose.

Eventually, Duane reached the Fabulous Beach. It, too, was snow-covered, making it indistinguishable from the rest of the icy landscape, but it still sloped at the perfect angle, so Duane flopped to the ground on his back and stared out at the Mainly Frozen Ocean. He felt at peace, free of care and still slightly dozy from his nap.

A glint from the direction of the Shipwreck caught Duane's attention. Duane was fairly certain it was the sunlight hitting C.C.'s metal telescope atop the slanted deck. He smiled and waved just in case C.C. was now watching him.

Minutes later, a tiny black spot arose in the sky above the Shipwreck, growing bigger and bigger as it came nearer. Soon Duane was able to see its wings and then C.C.'s big eyes. She landed beside him on the snow.

"Hello, C.C. It's good to see you."

"I will not stay long, Duane the polar bear. There is work to get back to."

"And what work is that?" asked Duane.

"I am conducting experiments for the advancement of knowledge toward the benefit of all," she replied. "What are you doing?"

"I am lying on the beach, licking an icicle pop and feeling the sunshine on my nose," said Duane. "Would you care to join me?" And before C.C. had time to answer, Duane broke the icicle in two and held out one half for her.

C.C. hesitated, not entirely sure what she should do. Perhaps you may think that taking the icicle pop is the obvious response, but C.C. was neither experienced nor comfortable in social situations. Unlike Handsome, for example, who was relaxed in both musk ox and *non*–musk ox interactions, C.C. could never quite grasp what was expected. Whether it was her inexperience that caused her discomfort or her discomfort that led to her inexperience remained to be proven. C.C. was still trying to figure out a proper experiment to examine it.

In the meantime, C.C. took a chance by accepting the half icicle pop from Duane, despite knowing that the icicle pop did not interest her in the least, as well as having to resist the temptation to point out that drinking a glass of water would be a much more efficient alternative with exactly the same benefits in nutrition. But then Duane smiled after she took the icicle pop, and C.C. gave a small, awkward smile in return. She knew she had made the right choice.

The owl and the polar bear stared out at the Mainly Frozen Ocean without speaking. The world was silent but for Duane's loud slurping and C.C.'s much quieter nibbling.

When Duane finished his icicle pop, he let out a great big sigh. C.C. again did not know how to respond. Sighs could mean many things. She looked over at Duane to study his face. "Are you disappointed, Duane the polar bear? Was the icicle pop not to your satisfaction?"

"Yes, it was. It was very delicious."

"Oh, then are you frustrated? Do you wish you had not shared half the icicle pop with me so that there would have been more deliciousness for you to enjoy?"

"Not at all. I was happy to share with you, C.C."

"Oh, then is it longing you feel? Do you fear that it was the last icicle pop you'll ever come across? Because I can tell you, that it is highly unlikely, scientifically speaking."

"I know, C.C. I'm sure there will be lots and lots of icicle pops this winter."

"Oh," said C.C. Her large eyes darted back and forth nervously. She'd exhausted all the explanations she could think of for Duane's sigh. Except for one. It was the one which made her heart feel heavy. "Then you sighed because you must be bored. I understand. I will leave you to your day."

C.C. positioned herself to push off into flight as Duane reached out to gently touch her wing. Gentle or not, the move startled C.C., who pulled away in defense. Duane immediately retracted his paw.

"I do not like to be touched, Duane the polar bear."

"I understand that now, C.C. And I'm sorry

for doing so," Duane added delicately. "But I wanted to say that I wasn't bored. I sighed because I was happy."

"There are happy sighs?"

"I believe so," replied Duane. Then he performed another sigh, but this time paying close attention to his feelings while he did it. "Yes, that was a happy sigh."

"Oh," said C.C. "I will make note of that."

"And I will remember not to touch."

The two friends held each other's gaze for a couple of blinks before returning once again to staring at the Mainly Frozen Ocean. This quiet spell lasted a good long time.

"Sometimes I like salty tastes," said Duane suddenly, apropos of nothing. "Not always, very little really, but sometimes."

C.C. was about to point out that salt is not something polar bears need to seek out in their diet and that another word for salt is "sodium" and the chemical element of sodium is Na and that polar bears will get their necessary dietary sodium just from the foods they eat, but she didn't because she was practicing listening.

"I've noticed," Duane continued, "that when the Mainly Frozen Ocean is just the Cold, Cold Ocean and I swim over to visit you, sometimes I can taste the salt in the water if I splash too much. But if I walk over to visit you when the Cold, Cold Ocean becomes the Mainly Frozen Ocean like it is now, and if I bend down to break a piece of the ice to eat, I can't taste the salt anymore."

C.C. controlled the urge to blurt out how most of the sea salt is forced down when the ice forms in winter so that the ocean water below the ice becomes dense with salt which makes it heavier and so it sinks. She also resisted explaining that if the salt *was* in the ice, there might not actually *be* ice because the salt lowers the freezing point by absorbing the energy from around it, causing the ice to melt. C.C. thought that all of this was very good information, but she still said nothing and continued listening.

"I guess what I'm saying," said Duane, "is that I love icicle pops—I really, really, really love icicle pops—but sometimes I wonder what it would be like to have icicle pops that taste different. Not always, but sometimes."

And this is when C.C. was glad she waited and listened before she spoke because she now knew she could offer something helpful to Duane. "Would you like to conduct some taste experiments, Duane the polar bear?"

"I think I would, C.C., but I don't know what that means exactly, so I can't say I would like it for sure."

"Fair enough," said the snowy owl. "Meet me at the Shipwreck, and I will show you what I had in mind."

C.C. flew off toward the Shipwreck while Duane walked across the Mainly Frozen Ocean, led by his growing curiosity. When he arrived in the windowed room at the back of the Shipwreck, C.C. had already set up the big wooden table with many items. There was a tray filled with icicles, a silver bowl, and a spoon. There was a pail with a mallet, a small dish, and three cups. The dish contained a pinch of salt. The three cups contained dried blackberries, huckleberries, and raspberries, all separately soaking in warm water.

"So what do I do, C.C.?" asked Duane, very intrigued.

"Let's begin with salt tasting because that was what started this. Grab an icicle and sprinkle some salt on it. I will take notes of what we learn."

Duane did exactly what C.C. instructed and then tasted his salt-flavored icicle pop. His face scrunched up tightly and his tongue was hanging out. "*Bleh*, I don't think I like that," he said.

"Duly noted," agreed C.C.

"Also, I think the salt made my icicle pop melt too soon."

"Well observed, Duane the polar bear," said C.C., which made Duane feel very proud. "Let's try the berries next. They've been soaking, so they will be juicy now."

"I like berries!" Duane said happily. But, as you can imagine, when he tried to add some raspberries onto the second long, thin icicle pop that he grabbed, they all quickly slid off.

C.C. had already predicted in her head that this might happen, which is why she had placed the other items on the table. "I would like to make a suggestion."

She then proceeded to guide Duane in the making of a new ice treat. The remaining icicles were put into the pail, and with the mallet, Duane hammered them and crushed them into something like snow, but still with the icy crunch he preferred. Duane scooped all of it into the silver bowl. This time when he added the berries, they all sat on the crushed ice along with their sweet juices. Duane picked up the spoon and dug in.

Oh, the smile that spread over Duane's face. This may have been the most delicious thing he had eaten in his entire life. Icy and juicy and sweet and crunchy, he closed his eyes and gave a long "mmmmmmm."

"Duly noted," said C.C. again.

Duane's eyes suddenly widened because he

finally understood what "conducting experiments for the advancement of knowledge toward the benefit of all" truly meant, and he was grateful. In fact, he was so grateful that his strongest impulse was to give C.C. a big hug as a way of saying thanks. He moved toward her, but then he stopped. He remembered that C.C. didn't like to be touched. So instead of a hug, he just looked at her and smiled and blinked three times. C.C. smiled and blinked three times back. For her, it was the perfect way to say "thank you" and "you're welcome."

Duane went back to eating his delicious new ice dessert, which he was inspired to call a Snow Delight. His eyes closed in the simple enjoyment of it. A large, loud sigh followed, but it did not come from Duane. This time it came from C.C., and Duane knew from the moment he heard it that it was a happy sigh.

6.
THE BIG BLIZZARD

ONE DAY, WHICH IS to say a Tuesday, because all stories involving unexpected situations take place on a Tuesday, Duane went exploring into unknown territory. He'd already explored down toward the ocean, and he'd already explored in the direction east of his cave, toward the river and beyond the river too—well, almost. But he'd never explored in the opposite direction. On this day, Duane would leave his cave, but instead of turning right, he would turn left and follow where his curiosity led.

Duane considered calling upon Handsome, his closest neighbor, to join in the adventure, but he was eager to start his exploring straightaway. With Handsome, if he didn't simply say no right off, then there were bound to be many preparations required. "One cannot just rush from one's home looking shabby, rumpled, and unkempt," Handsome would likely say to Duane. "One never knows who one might run into, and appearances matter." By the time Handsome had finished his face-washing, his hair-brushing, and his eyebrow-tweaking, it would already be noon, and lunch would demand attention. *No*, thought Duane, *this exploring will be best done on my own.*

So Duane headed left, and that was that.

He walked at a fast clip, feeling quite excited

because this was, after all, an excursion into the unchartered and unfamiliar. He might discover a new river or an old mountain or a glacier of dubious age. He might find a variety of ice perfectly suited for Snow Delights. *That* possibility was suggested by Duane's stomach, which was never shy to voice an opinion. But what if he was to encounter some danger along the way in this unknown territory? Imagine stumbling upon monsters. Snarling things, hissing things, croaking things! Things that spout fire and smoke, as shown in C.C.'s books! Monsters like that. Thinking about possible encounters with danger made Duane feel brave. And feeling both excited *and* brave put a bigger bounce in Duane's step, which kept him going into the unknown territory for quite some time. He was alert and ready for anything.

On and on he went. And then on and on he went some more.

Eventually, the bounce lessened to a dribble, and then the dribble sputtered to a trickle, until it finally reduced back to his usual lumbering step. It became more and more evident to Duane that nothing interesting was going to happen. No rivers, no mountains, no Snow Delights or monsters. The snowy land was ever so flat and uninspiring and went on forever without a glimmer of adventure beckoning over the horizon. Nor did Duane make any new acquaintances along the way, either passing by or flying overhead, which would have certainly brightened up the experience.

Duane stopped and sighed.

"Oh well," he said to himself.

"Too bad," agreed his stomach.

But this was a Tuesday, as I mentioned, and Tuesdays are for unexpected situations, by which I mean that the sky suddenly sagged heavier with clouds laden with trouble, while the wind, feeling mischievous, grew increasingly more powerful. The temperature dropped to a most inhospitable level. Snow started falling in copious amounts, which was then quickly lifted up by the wind so that it fell again and again in swirling waves, blotting out the sun, leaving Duane alone within a ferocious, howling blizzard.

"Oh dear," said Duane to himself.

His stomach had nothing to add.

There are mornings when you wake up thinking it's a great day for exploring and it turns out that you were correct. There are other mornings when you wake up thinking that it's a great day for exploring and by afternoon, you wished the thought hadn't even crossed your mind. Duane found himself among the latter category of mornings.

Whoosh! blew the wind.

Click-click-click-click! chattered Duane's teeth in reply.

The temperature dropped so low that even with his thick fur, Duane shivered in the gasping, biting cold. His eyelids were freezing together, and soon they would be bound shut as ice pellets whipped his face from all directions. His muscles ached. His energy was seeping out of him. Duane was exposed and vulnerable to a most dangerous situation.

Shelter was required. Duane's blizzard-addled brain was able to muster at least that much of a plan. So he dug and dug into the rising snow with the goal of hollowing out a snow cave, a place to weather the terrible storm. It was hard work. His arms were stiffening. He was tiring so quickly. His big, strong paws would soon fail him. Duane grunted and moaned, and just when he thought he was making some progress in digging his cave, he came up against a sturdy wall of snow buried within the snow. Duane was confused. He clawed at the wall, creating a peephole. Through Duane's near-frozen-shut eyes, he saw a flicker of fire. His nostrils picked up the smell of smoke. His ears were suddenly assaulted by a discord of barks and growls.

Oh my, thought Duane. *Have I stumbled up against the lair of one of those flame-breathing dragon monsters?* He vividly remembered the frightening picture that C.C. had shown him.

What was he to do? Without shelter, he would surely freeze, but protection from the terrible cold lay within the home of some fright-ful creature. Duane had come to a dilemma often described as being stuck between a rock and a hard place. In Duane's case, he was stuck between a blizzard and a dragon monster.

In the last remaining non-addled corner of his blizzard-frozen brain, Duane reasoned with himself. *I left the protection of my cave this morning as an explorer. As an explorer, is not my job to explore the unknown? And even if that unknown is scary or dangerous, don't I, as an explorer, still have to explore it, especially if it's a matter of life and death?*

These were very good questions best answered by a less freezing polar bear. But more importantly, what the questions did do was make Duane feel brave and heroic by asking them. With all the strength he could gather, Duane clawed at the snow wall until he forced his way into the lair, ready to face his unknown fate at the mercy of the dragon monster. "I am Duane!" he shouted valiantly. "Polar bear explorer in search of the unknown *and* a little warmth, if possible!"

But there was no dragon monster before him.

There was, however, a young girl in a bright red parka, tending to a fire in the middle of a cozy ice dome. Eight sled dogs sat attentively beside her.

A short pause followed Duane's dramatic entry in which Duane took in the nonthreatening surroundings and lowered his front paws, while at the same time, the eight sled dogs relaxed onto their stomachs and the young girl simply blinked twice. You or I might have responded to a polar bear crashing into our home with a little more alarm, perhaps. I won't speak for you, but I would definitely have screamed at least once, or five times. The young girl, however, did not. She was placid and calm. The world may well be filled with all sorts of surprises, but she was not one to be surprised when she encountered any of them. "There was a perfectly fine entrance on the other side," she eventually said, indicating the snow tunnel behind her.

Duane glanced around her and nodded. "I realize that now," he said apologetically. "Perhaps I should fill in the extra hole I made."

"I think the storm will do it on its own in very little time," said the girl. "If you don't mind me saying, you look rather cold and tired. Come sit by the fire until the weather decides to be friendlier and we can all go about our day."

That was the best suggestion Duane had heard in a long time. He flopped down onto the ground with his face near enough to the fire to thaw his ice-covered nose but not burn it. It was snug and warm in the cozy snow cave while the wind howled and raged. This time, it sounded as if the monster were on the outside.

"I was exploring unknown territory," Duane explained to his host. "I thought nothing interesting was ever going to happen, and then this happened."

The young girl in the red parka gave a quick nod of understanding. "Tuesdays," she said.

"Tuesdays," agreed Duane.

The ten souls passed the time in friendly conversation. The girl shared dried berries with Duane, which kept his stomach content and well-behaved. The sled dogs, who referred to themselves as the Pack, volunteered to sing a few choral pieces consisting of a lot of yips and howls. Their songs touched Duane. They made him feel wistful and homesick for his cave and his friends. Sleepiness eventually came over all of them, and without needing to announce it, they all lay close to the fire, close to one another, and slumbered peacefully while the wind's angry tirade lessened.

In the morning, Duane volunteered to clear the snow that blocked the girl's tunnel entrance and all the snow that had accumulated beyond it too. Outside, the sky was blue and the sun was shining again. The ignored wind, its feelings hurt, had already left in search of another audience.

The girl loaded up her sled before turning to Duane to say goodbye. She felt like a friend now, and Duane was always compelled to hug his friends with all his heart, but what if she was the sort who preferred three blinks, like C.C.? As Duane fretted over how to say a proper farewell that contained all his gratitude and happiness and sadness, too, in their separating, he didn't notice that the girl had already stretched her arms as much as they would reach around his waist and laid the side of her head against his fur.

"Ah," said Duane gently, and gently, too, he hugged her back.

Shortly after, he watched the devoted Pack carry the girl in the red parka in the opposite direction from where he was heading. The girl never told Duane her name, but since Duane was good at giving names, he chose to call her

Sun Girl, for different reasons, some of them which you might be able to figure out. It would not be the last time Duane would meet Sun Girl, but he didn't know that yet. He turned toward home, his exploring adventure concluded. He looked forward to reaching his cave and his soft bed. He looked forward, too, to telling his other friends about his new friends, and how they had all coped with the unexpected situation.

7.
WHEN DUANE FIRST MET MAGIC

D UANE HAD BEEN REQUESTED to attend
an afternoon tea hosted by his friend
Handsome. The official invitation, which Duane
found lying at the lip of his cave, said as much:

You are cordially invited to an afternoon tea
at the residence of Handsome the musk ox,
Esquire, who will host the affair with aplomb
and watercress sandwiches, as well as fruit
sorbets, shortbread, and tarts. It shall take

place three days hence at two o'clock.

RSVP at your earliest convenience.

Duane was both excited and nervous upon reading it. The consuming of sorbets, tarts, and aplomb sounded like a wonderful way to pass an afternoon, but the mysterious RSVP left Duane unsure of what to do. He tried saying RSVP out loud a few times, thinking he'd recognize the word if he heard it. "Risvip. Ris-si-vi-pip." It did not help.

What did help was when he turned the invitation over. As if Handsome could read Duane's mind, he had written on the back:

RSVP is short for "répondez s' il vous plaît,"
which is French for: you must tell me if you
can make it, Duane, otherwise all my great
efforts will have been wasted.

Mystery solved, Duane now had to walk all the way to Handsome's residence, which was an open field due north, in order to tell Handsome that he would return in three days' time to attend the afternoon tea. Secretly, Duane wished they could have the afternoon tea this day, since he was already walking over there. To his way of thinking, it would have been more efficient. But Handsome was a friend, and Duane knew that Handsome preferred, as he put it, *to obey the rules and etiquette of society in regard to the decorum of social gatherings both big and small*. Duane was not completely sure what any of that meant, but he did know that if there were to be sorbets, tarts, and aplomb to eat, it would have to wait for three more days.

The way to Handsome's place passed between two long but short hills, now completely covered in fresh sparkly snow. Looking at all the beautiful wintry scenes of snow and ice made Duane's heart beat strong and happily. So different from Handsome's experience of the season, because winter meant that the reflection pond in the middle of his field was covered over in snow. Idle days of standing at the water's edge staring down at his striking face would have to wait until the spring thaw. Duane suspected that Handsome was feeling a little lonely without his reflection to keep him company and that's why Handsome was having an afternoon tea.

But as Duane continued down the path, he heard a hello coming from a snowbank.

"Hello," said the snowbank.

Duane had never before been addressed by a hill, snow-covered or otherwise. Up until then, he would have confidently said that hills do not speak. But the hill that had said hello, said hello again.

"Hello."

"Hello to you," replied Duane.

The snowbank said nothing further. The snowbank had, in effect, returned to being a silent snowbank. Duane decided it was for the best. He had begun to take his leave when he heard a hello coming from the opposite snowbank.

"Hello," said the second snowbank in much the same voice as the first.

"Hmm." Duane paused. Because he was recently thinking about Handsome's rules of manners and etiquette, he wondered if perhaps there was a proper way to address a hill, or any other geographical feature.

"How do you do?" was the reply Duane tried on.

The snowbank blinked, or maybe twinkled for a split second. Duane wasn't sure, but other than that, it remained quiet.

It would seem that "How do you do?" isn't correct either,

Duane thought. Continuing on his way, he was greeted by both snowbanks, over and over, first on one side, then the other, sometimes high up on the hill, sometimes at the bottom. Duane offered as many different replies as he could.

"Hello."

"Hi?"

"Hello."

"Greetings?"

"Hello."

"Good morning?"

"Hello."

"Um . . . hey there?"

"Hello."

"Sorry, I really must be going."

Duane tried to be civil, but in truth, he felt a little spooked, so he quickened his pace more and more until soon he was running away.

When he reached the field that his friend called home, Duane confirmed his RSVP to the afternoon tea, which Handsome much appreciated, and then recounted how he had been spoken to over and over by two snow-covered hills, which Handsome did not appreciate.

"I trust you're not going daft, Duane," he said impatiently. "I had an uncle who went daft. The amusement runs thin sooner than one might think. I don't wish to go to the effort of serving you afternoon tea if you're just going to wear the teacup on your head like a bonnet and recite limerick poems."

"Is that what your daft uncle did?" asked Duane, genuinely curious. "Do you remember any of the poems?"

Handsome let out an involuntary snicker before he regained his stiff composure and severely said, "No, I do not. And even if I did, it would be most improper to repeat them. Now, if you would be so kind, I have an afternoon tea to prepare for."

Duane was not keen on returning home the same way as he came because he feared that there would be more hellos to contend with from the hills. So he decided to take the long way around, and as he was taking the long way around, it occurred to him that he was now close to the Mainly Frozen Cold Ocean and the Shipwreck where C.C. lived.

"If anyone would know how to greet a geographical feature, it would be her," he said.

Duane reached the shoreline and crossed the Mainly Frozen Cold Ocean until he reached the jagged gash in the bow of the Shipwreck that served as a door. He entered and made his way toward the back of the ship, up the stairs, until he came to a room. Duane poked his head through the doorway. C.C. was perched on a wooden table, looking down at a large open book.

"Hello, C.C. May I interrupt your reading with a question?"

"You already have."

"Excuse me?"

"And again."

Duane was momentarily confused until he realized that by asking if he could ask a question, he was asking a question. "Oh, I see." He tried again. "May I interrupt your reading with a question *after* the question I'm asking right now?"

"Yes," replied C.C. curtly.

"How does one greet a snow-covered hill?"

C.C. blinked her two big eyes twice. "The short answer is, you don't. Now, allow me to ask you a question, Duane the polar bear. Why would you want to greet a snow-covered hill?"

Grateful that C.C.'s question wasn't hard, as they often were, Duane wasted no time in answering. "Because it said hello to me. Or rather, two hills said hello to me. Many times over, I might add."

C.C. stared at Duane, this time without blinking. She let a brief sigh escape. It was not a sigh of contentment. "Hills, like all other geographical features, are not in the custom of speaking hellos or anything else."

"That's what I thought too, C.C.!" agreed Duane with great relief. "I said to myself, 'Duane, hills or mountains or icebergs do not talk.' But then they did."

C.C. strode across the big oak table toward Duane and pointed one of her wing tips at him. "You haven't considered the possibility that there may be another more reasonable explanation for the voices you heard."

"More reasonable?" asked Duane. He paused to mull that consideration over. Then suddenly his face brightened. "Of course!" he shouted happily. "Talking hills? What was I thinking? It must have simply been magic."

C.C. bowed her head and shook it slowly in a disappointed manner that put Duane's newly acquired relief into question. "It wasn't magic?" he asked timidly.

"Duane the polar bear, I am a scientist, as you well know. I deal with what is. I cannot accept that magic is involved. Bring over that chunk of lapis lazuli that's sitting on the shelf. I have something you can use for your next encounter with the voices."

The now-chagrined polar bear obediently retrieved the blue rock and followed all her instructions, which included using a mortar and pestle to crush the rock into a fine blue powder, pouring the powder into a flask, and capping it with a cork. C.C. then explained what he was to do with it when the time came.

"Thank you, C.C.," said Duane, feeling again relieved. The snowy owl went back to her studies, and Duane took his leave as quietly as possible so as to disturb her no further.

As he walked along the ship's corridor past doorways that led into rooms filled with pretty objects, including porcelain plates and decorative silverware, Duane was reminded of Handsome's afternoon tea in three days' time. It occurred to him that it might be a proper gesture to bring along a gift. He recalled Handsome mentioning it in one of his many lectures on manners. Duane chose a room and rummaged through it for a good long time until he came across an item that he was sure Handsome would like. He even found a small case to present it in. So with his flask of blue powder and the box containing his present, Duane headed home.

Three days later, as the invitation had stated, Duane spruced himself up for what he hoped would be a tasty assortment of treats. He grabbed Handsome's present, which he also spruced up by tying a bright yellow ribbon around it, and left his cave. A minute later, he returned to the cave to take along the flask of blue powder. "Just in case," he told himself.

When Duane reached the point along the path that took him between the two snowy hills, his body tensed in expectation of invisible voices surrounding him again. He didn't hear a peep. Out of curiosity, he slowed down and listened extra hard. Still, not a voice made itself known. This might have given Duane a degree of comfort if it weren't for the fact that while he was listening, the bright yellow ribbon around Handsome's gift was untying all by itself before Duane's very eyes. *This is even worse than hills saying hello*, he thought while watching the loose ribbon inexplicably fall to the ground. Duane jumped back in fear.

"Hello," said a voice behind him.

Duane jumped forward in fear.

"Hello," said the voice just to his right.

At the same time that Duane jumped left in fear, a loud "Ah!" escaped his lips. Duane was as scared as if he had seen a ghost, which, as it turns out, is what he assumed he saw. Keeping what few wits he still had left about him, Duane flipped the cork off the flask and flung the contents in the direction of the voice just as C.C. had instructed him to do. A large cloud of blue powder hung in the air. But as the powder settled, Duane could observe the outline of a creature. It was small and furry, with rounded ears and a snout. I can tell you now that it was an arctic fox whose fur, generally speaking, is as white as snow, making it extremely difficult to spot in the winter. However, at that moment, its fur was now as blue as the lapis lazuli powder it was covered in.

"Why did you go and do that?" demanded the fox, most displeased.

"Because I was frightened," Duane explained. "You scared me."

"Oh, come on! It was just a joke!" shouted the fox, a little too dramatically, all things considered. "I just wanted to have a little fun!"

"It wasn't fun for me," insisted Duane. "I thought I was going daft. I thought I might end up wearing a teacup on my head and spouting limerick poems."

"All right, fine! I get it! It wasn't a nice thing to do to a stranger. I'm sorry," said the fox, slumping herself onto the ground, again very dramatically, and placing her paw to her forehead

as if to suggest she'd just had the most exhausting day. "But now I'm blue, so we're even."

If this was the fox's way of apologizing, it was unrecognizable to Duane. It almost felt as if Duane should feel bad about being scared. More than that, Duane's nerves were still on edge. "Where are all the others?"

The fox, who was still on the ground sighing heavily under the burden of being misunderstood, suddenly stopped and raised her head. "What others?"

"The first time we met, I heard hellos coming from both sides of the path, atop the hills and near the bottom. Just now, my ribbon was untied in front of me, then a voice spoke behind me, and then you spoke to my right. Where are all the others?"

The blue fox was back up on her feet, bouncing in front of Duane in sheer delight.

"Yes! Lovely! Excellent! *You* thought there were others? *You* thought there was more than yours truly?"

Duane nodded cautiously at the sudden bundle of energy. "That is what I thought."

"Ooh, yes! Wonderful! But the thing is . . . the most excellent thing . . . the thing that I must tell you, so you will be absolutely amazed is . . . it *is* just me!" The fox stood still long enough to point to herself with a big, proud smile.

"Really?" asked Duane, as amazed as the fox had predicted.

"Yes! Yes! Let me show you!" The fox now worked herself into a tizzy of motion. "This is where I live! Under this hill and that hill! I have secret doors everywhere!" To demonstrate this, for the next minute, she proceeded to zip into invisible holes and then pop out of other holes at a speed nearly impossible to follow. Duane found himself turning one way, then spinning quickly around barely in time to see the fox dash between his legs and disappear into yet another hole. None of this would have been observable to his eye were it not for the lapis lazuli powder that allowed him to see flashes of the blue fox set against the white snow.

Duane had lost his fear. He was overtaken by another feeling equally as strong. He felt awe. What the fox showed him proved to be the reasonable explanation to the voices that C.C. assured him there would be, but nonetheless, to Duane, the illusion the fox created seemed magical. Now that he saw how it was done, he almost wished he could go back to not knowing.

"So, you see—you do see, don't you? It was just me doing all this by myself!" exclaimed the fox, with her arms stretched out wide.

"I do," agreed Duane. He stood there pondering the fox. Since he'd arrived in the Very, Very Far North from somewhere else, he'd made many friends: C.C. and Handsome, Sun Girl and the Pack. Could this fox become a friend too? A friend like her would never be boring, Duane thought. But a friend like that, he suspected, could also be exhausting. It would have to be, as C.C. often said, one of those wait-and-see situations, he finally decided. In the meantime, there was the afternoon tea.

"I was just on my way to my friend's place. His name is Handsome. My name is Duane. Would you care to join me?"

"I would like to. I mean, I would really, really love to go! But there is the question of my blueness. I'm not blue by nature. It would give the completely wrong impression!"

Duane assured the fox that he would explain

everything and that it might even make an entertaining story to tell while eating sorbets, tarts, and aplomb. The prodding eventually did the trick. While Duane walked to Handsome's place, the fox bounced and ran and occasionally disappeared and reappeared beside him.

When they arrived, it was clear that Handsome took his hosting duties seriously. In the middle of the snowy field was a table, beautifully set with a tablecloth, fancy dishes and cups, and a four-tiered serving tray filled with the most mouthwatering treats Duane had ever seen in his life. The fox bounced around the table, equally enthralled. Handsome studied her solemnly.

"Who is your blue friend?" he asked Duane.

"I don't know yet," replied Duane. "I do know that she isn't actually blue. And I hope you don't mind that I invited her without asking."

Because Handsome knew that a host must always be gracious, he said nothing other than "Well, I suppose we'll need another chair, won't we?" But if there were any feelings of ill will, they melted away when Duane handed him the present, complete with the yellow ribbon bow.

Handsome untied the bow and opened the case. He gasped. Duane had brought him a hand mirror with an ornately carved wooden handle.

"For the winter months," Duane explained, "when the reflection pond is frozen over and covered in snow."

"Yes," said Handsome, deeply moved, not just by his striking image in the mirror, but by the thoughtful gesture of Duane's gift. "Yes," he said again, looking this time at Duane. "Thank you."

"When are we going to eat?" exclaimed the fox in the overly dramatic fashion that seemed to be how she expressed everything. "I am SO starved! I'm famished! If I don't eat soon, I may simply die on the spot!"

"Well, we certainly don't want that to happen," said Handsome, pulling himself together.

"Duane, if you'd be so kind as to fetch another chair, I will pour the tea for us all."

And thus began the afternoon tea shared

between two friends and a blue fox who wasn't actually blue, and in fact would stop being blue once she went home and washed, but she *was* still an arctic fox, soon to be named Magic.

8.
MAGIC GOES TOO FAR

EVER SINCE THE DAY that Magic the arctic fox became friends with Duane, she'd been coming to his cave. When she dropped by in the morning, Magic would often discover that Duane hadn't yet awoken, and by "often," I mean all the time, because Duane tended to sleep in.

"Come on, Duane!" she would holler while attempting to prod him off his mattress.

"Hmm? Ah-mmmm-zzzzzz," Duane would semi-reply.

It was fortunate for Duane that he was such a sound sleeper and far too big for an arctic fox to push out of bed because Magic would eventually give up and leave. But not before sighing dramatically and exclaiming, "How does someone waste the day like that? I mean—really!" to which Duane would reply, "Mmmm-ah-phu-zzzzzz," followed by two loud snorts.

On the occasions that Magic visited later in the day, when he was awake, Duane found himself overwhelmed by her energy and exuberance.

"Finally, you're up! Well, it's about time. Do you know what I've been doing the whole while you've been snoozing away? Do you? Never mind asking because it would take another hour to list everything off."

"Okay," he would reply unsteadily.

Duane wasn't sure how he was supposed to respond to Magic when she went on like that. Then again, it didn't really seem to matter *if* he responded either. "What are you having for breakfast?" she might ask. And no sooner than Duane would reply with an "Oh, I don't know, maybe I'll have a bowl of—" Magic would cut him off with an "I jumped as high as a musk ox the other day! I landed right on Handsome's back. You wouldn't think it possible, but I totally did it." And no sooner than Duane would reply with a "That sounds like quite a high jump indeed," Magic would have moved on to the topic of home renovations for a fox hole. Duane gathered that Magic didn't have a long attention span.

Duane once asked Handsome how *he* handled conversations with Magic because she would drop by his field whenever Duane was still asleep in his cave. Handsome didn't have any advice to give. Handsome never even noticed that she was talking to him, as he was generally too preoccupied with his reflection in his new hand mirror. The only time he was made aware of Magic's presence was the day she jumped on his back. "I am not a fan of surprise acrobatics," he told Duane. "One should not be used as a pommel horse without fair warning. It's simply good manners."

Magic was a puzzle to Duane. In some ways she was loud and bossy and not always considerate, but on the other hand she was so full of energy and fun and playful.

"I was thinking, Duane," she might say, always poking him in the ticklish part of his belly whenever she said his name, "wouldn't it be amazing if you, Duane (*poke*), and I could fly? Wouldn't it, Duane (*poke*)?"

By the third Duane-poke, he would be giggling and helpless, but he would also be intrigued by the idea. "To fly like C.C.? To look down on the Very, Very Far North from the sky? Oh, yes, I think that would be amazing."

Meanwhile, Magic would be running circles around him, shouting happily, "Never mind flying like C.C.! How about flying like me?" and then she would throw herself into the air with her front paws spread out like wings, forcing Duane to react quickly and catch her. The power of her throw would cause him to fall onto the ground on his back. "That, Duaney-Duane (*poke, poke*), is how a flying fox flies," she would say, grinning with mischief.

On the day that Duane brought her over to the Shipwreck to meet C.C. for the first time, it was clear that this was not a good idea at all. Before C.C. had the opportunity to study

Magic's face, the arctic fox was running all about her room, opening jars without asking, knocking over C.C.'s research papers, and spilling chemicals that required C.C. to quickly open more windows for ventilation. To say that Magic ruffled C.C.'s feathers was both an understatement and a statement of fact because at one point she came up to C.C. and said, "Can you really fly with those wings? I mean—really! If I had wings, they would have much longer feathers than those." As hurtful as those comments were, what made things worse was that as she said them, Magic was lifting up C.C.'s wings and looking under them. Duane gasped in horror, knowing how much C.C. did not like being touched. He rushed over to steer Magic out of C.C.'s room at once, giving C.C. a weak apologetic smile before closing the door shut.

"Well, that was a nice visit!" declared Magic,

demonstrating she had no awareness of her behavior.

The story that I am about to tell you begins right after those words were spoken. Duane wanted to explain to Magic how C.C. would prefer contact of the nonphysical variety, but before he got two words out of his mouth, she was bounding down the Shipwreck's corridor peeking into all the other rooms. This led into an unplanned game of hide-and-seek in which Duane was trying to find Magic among all the boxes and strange objects, and Magic was sneaking up behind Duane to poke him in the back before rushing off to hide again. The game only stopped because Magic came across a strange object that caught her attention.

"What's that?" she asked Duane when he joined her in the room that contained the strange object.

Had Magic asked him about most any of the other items that filled the rooms, Duane would have had to confess that he didn't know what they were. But Magic was looking at a long object made of wooden slats nailed together that curled back on themselves at one end. And because Duane had been curious about the same object on one of his earlier trips to the Shipwreck and had asked C.C. the very same question, he knew what the object was.

"It's a toboggan," he replied. "According to C.C., you can use it to pull supplies along the ice."

"Or according to me," Magic said with a twinkle in her eyes, "you could use it to slide down a hill really, really fast!"

A smile grew on Duane's face as he imagined it. "I suppose you could."

"Duaney-Duane (*poke, poke*), we've got ourselves an adventure!"

So Duane carried the toboggan off the Shipwreck and pulled it along the Mainly Frozen Cold Ocean toward the snowy shore. Magic sometimes sat on the toboggan while Duane pulled, and she sometimes ran around Duane when she couldn't sit still any longer because she was too excited thinking about going downhill.

"Let's try it on Whaleback Hill!" she said, referring to the hill well-named because it indeed looked just like a whale's back.

"All right," agreed Duane.

"No, scratch that! Let's try it on Double Whaleback Hill!" Magic said, referring to another hill also well-named because it looked like two whales stacked on top of each other.

"All right, I guess," Duane agreed, slightly less confident.

"No, wait!" shouted Magic, stopping right in

front of Duane with her paws out. "*Not* Double Whaleback Hill!"

"Not Double Whaleback Hill?" Duane asked.

Magic's voice got very low and very serious-sounding. "No, Duane (*poke*), what we must go down . . . what we absolutely, without a chance of changing our minds, must go down is . . . Baby Whaleback Hill."

You may be thinking, and quite rightly, that after suggesting Whaleback Hill, followed by Double Whaleback Hill, to then suggest tobogganing down something called Baby Whaleback Hill would be somewhat less exciting, not more. You would be wrong. Baby Whaleback Hill resembled not one but one *hundred* baby whales piled together in a giant pyramid shape. It was monstrously tall and covered with endless bumps and bulges from top to bottom. Why it wasn't called the Mountain of One Hundred

Baby Whales just goes to show that not everyone is as good at giving names as Duane is. In any case, Duane's concern about Magic's suggestion was because of what the hill *was*, and not what it was called.

"I don't know, Magic. Baby Whaleback Hill could be too much for us to handle."

"Ugh! Come on! I mean—really!" Magic was working herself up into an exceptionally over-dramatic outrage. "Duane! We've dragged a very heavy toboggan all the way from the Shipwreck, and I've come up, on my own, with the most brilliant idea for an adventure. Please do not tell me that you intend to let these great efforts all go to waste! Hmm, Duane? You're not telling me that, are you?"

The force of Magic's determination was like a hurricane gale. It pinned Duane's will into submission. Even though he knew that it had

only been him who pulled the very heavy toboggan, he didn't feel able to speak up. Even though
Duane had very serious concerns about the plan
that Magic was suggesting, he didn't feel strong
enough to argue. "No," he replied sheepishly,
"I'm not telling you that."

"Good! So let's get climbing!" declared
Magic happily, as if her last outburst hadn't even
happened.

Following Magic's lead, Duane pulled the
toboggan up the steep side of Baby Whaleback
Hill. They climbed and climbed the snow-
covered mountain, reaching a level that was
already above both Whaleback and Double
Whaleback Hills. But before Duane could set the
toboggan down for their great adventure ride to
begin, Magic stuck out her paw to stop him.

"Higher!" she said.

Duane gulped. "Higher?"

Magic gave him a mischievous grin before bouncing up the mountainside. Obediently, Duane followed, with his heart beating faster, not just from the exertion of climbing the mountain but from the mounting fear inside him. When he finally caught up to Magic, he again started to set down the toboggan before being stopped.

"Higher!" Magic insisted.

"But," Duane attempted weakly, "isn't this too much?"

"Come on, Duaney-Duane (*poke, poke*), we're nearly there!"

The voice inside Duane was trying to get his attention, trying to tell him to stop and insist that they go back down. But Duane was not listening to that voice, even though he'd known and trusted that voice for as long as he could remember. Magic's voice was stronger, more convincing, and more confident. Magic's voice held the promise of excitement and adventure. Duane followed that voice farther up the steep mountainside as if he were under a spell.

They reached an elevation that looked down upon the Very, Very Far North, with a few clouds actually hanging below them and the Shipwreck nothing but a speck seen far off in the distance. "Here!" declared Magic, pointing at a spot for Duane to place the toboggan. Anxiously, he did, and then he sat down on it.

"I will sit in the front," insisted Magic, "because I want to experience the complete thrill of the ride! Are you ready, Duane?"

"No, not really," said Duane, quietly but honestly.

"Well, ready or not, here we go!" Magic yanked both of Duane's arms, causing him to bend forward and so creating just enough weight on the front end of the toboggan to tip it into motion. They were off, heading down the terrifyingly steep incline, picking up speed with each passing second.

Bump!

"Whoa!" they both cried after hitting the first of many knobs and swells along the way.

Bump, ka-bump, ka-bump-bump-bump!

"Whoa!" cried Duane again, this time on his own.

They were barely staying on the toboggan. Each bump lifted them a few inches above it so that it gave Duane a true sensation of flying, or maybe just falling—falling very quickly from a very tall height. In any case, it was a new feeling. The great fear Duane had as they climbed up the mountain was being overtaken and replaced by something more powerful: the feeling of exhilaration. The ride was reckless and wild; it was

madness! But as the seconds continued, with the
toboggan still rushing down at supersonic speed
and the bumps still tossing them up again and
again, they still hadn't crashed, and this created
in Duane an odd sense of security. *Maybe it's going
to be okay after all*, he thought.

Bump, ka-bump-bump, ka-bump-bump-ka-bump!

Each bounce fed Duane a jolt of electricity.
There he was, rushing down a mountainside,
with the whole world blurring around him. He

felt unstoppable, invincible. He gave in to the excitement. "Whooo-heeeee!" he shouted with glee.

Bumpity-bumpity, bump-ka-bump, bump-ka-bump!

"Whooo-heee!" Duane shouted louder. "Magic, isn't this fun?"

It was then that he noticed how quiet Magic had become. Since she was sitting in front of Duane, he couldn't see how big her eyes had grown shortly after they pushed off the edge. He couldn't see how hard she was clenching her teeth and how hard she was both grasping and pushing against the curl of the toboggan as they hurled through the thrilling ride that was, as she had pointed out earlier, her own brilliant idea. Magic didn't speak because Magic was in the deep throes of terror.

But then Magic did speak. It wasn't loud at first because it was directed more to herself than to Duane. "I can't I can't I can't I can't I can't I can't I can't I can't . . ."

"What?" asked Duane.

"I can't I can't I can't I can't I can't I can't I can't I can't I can't . . ."

"What was that?" Duane was straining to hear above the *whoosh* of the toboggan sliding over the snow and ice.

"I can't I can't I can't I can't I can't I can't I can't I can't I can't . . ."

"Magic, you have to speak louder!"

And then Magic did speak louder, at the top of her voice, in fact. "I CAN'T DO THIS, DUANE!" she screamed, just before she tossed herself off the side of the toboggan.

Time instantly expanded—at least it did for Duane, at that moment. The world relaxed into a slow, steady beat, like the drip of an icicle on a cold, cloudy day. Duane twisted his neck around, following Magic's sudden departure, watching the whole unexpected episode unravel before his eyes in slow motion. Magic jumped, and then she tumbled head over heels once, then twice, then three and a half times, until she came to a complete stop on her back, splayed onto the snow like a fox-shaped cookie cutter. The last thing Duane saw as he continued to plummet down the steep mountainside was Magic sitting up, giving herself a shake, and then waving cheerfully at Duane without a care in the world.

It was a happy image. Duane gave a sigh of relief for Magic while he turned toward the front of the toboggan, toward the portion of the thrilling adventure ride that was still unfinished and awaiting. And at the very moment he did turn back around, time snapped like a stretched elastic band. It returned Duane back to the ridiculous speed of the runaway toboggan that was hurtling him down the side of Baby Whaleback Hill (so badly named, all things considered), and the fear that Duane had set aside earlier, so as not to spoil the fun, was back now, bigger than ever. Duane was very, very afraid, and to top it off, he was now all alone.

Bump, thump, thumpity-bump, ka-bump-bump-thump!

Oh dear oh dear oh dear, thought Duane. *This will surely be the end of me. Why did I listen to Magic?*

Bump, thump, thumpity-bump, THUMP!

The toboggan hit a much larger protrusion that sent it, along with Duane, high into the air and on a slant, as well. Duane had to lean over to the opposite side to bring the toboggan squarely back onto the snow. *THUD!* Duane averted what might have been a terrible crash, but the thrilling ride didn't slow down. Even if he'd had the wits about him to jump off the toboggan like Magic, he couldn't. There was no time. The big thumps were coming one after another now. *Bumpity-THUMP! Bumpity-THUMP!* Duane was leaning every which way to keep the toboggan upright and to keep himself from injury. The *THUDS* of the toboggan hitting the ground each time felt so hard. Duane was bruised and sore all over.

Just below him but approaching very fast was the bottom of Baby Whaleback Hill. If he could hold on a little bit longer, there would be an end to the scariest thing he had ever done in his life. The gentle comfort of hope in Duane's heart could only be felt in tiny spurts in between the *THUMPS!* and *THUDS!* But steadily, steadily, the steep incline did level off. Duane was not going down so much as going straight. Yes! This was indeed a true moment of hope and relief for the poor polar bear, or at least it would have been but for two things: the toboggan had barely slowed down at all, and directly in its path was the much smaller, but still not insignificant, Whaleback Hill.

Duane and the toboggan shot up Whaleback Hill with the gracefulness of a swooping bird. After they quickly reached the summit and then went up and over the hill, it was as if Duane had been launched into space. He truly was flying now. There was nothing but sky around him. Higher and higher the toboggan went, but also slower and slower. For a brief moment, Duane experienced absolute silence, which was peaceful but also dreadful, because that was the moment that he and the toboggan, so far above the ground below, finally stopped.

After that, it was all about falling. Duane let go of the toboggan because there really was no purpose in them staying together at this point. He wished the toboggan well and then focused on his own descent. As he was very high in the air, there was plenty of time for him to think before he hit the earth, so he did. *I really don't think I'm as much of an adventuring polar bear as I am an exploring polar bear,* Duane considered. *I should try to remember that if I live through today. But if I don't survive, I wish to acknowledge how much I will miss my friends, C.C., Handsome, and even Magic. Oh, and let's not forget Sun Girl and the Pack. Speaking of which, isn't that Sun Girl and the Pack just below me? What are they holding, I wonder?*

The answer to the last question that Duane managed to ask was that they were holding a large blanket by the edges, all of them—Sun Girl using her hands, and each member of the Pack using their teeth. The blanket was stretched out as tight as they could pull.

PHUMP! Duane hit the center of the stretched blanket.

BOING! Duane bounced off the stretched blanket.

THUD! Duane landed decisively, but safely, in a patch of nearby snow.

The very much alive polar bear stayed in the snow on his back as Sun Girl and the Pack gathered around him.

"You've been having an adventure, Duane," said Sun Girl.

"I have," agreed Duane. "I tobogganed down Baby Whaleback Hill."

"We saw you," said the Pack in unison.

"It's not very well-named," Duane suggested.

"We agree," said Sun Girl and every member of the Pack but one, who blushed and looked embarrassed. "It's more of a mountain."

"I shouldn't have gone down it," said Duane. "It was dangerous, and I knew it was dangerous, but I pretended that I had forgotten. I was trying to impress a friend."

Sun Girl nodded in understanding. "How did that work out?"

It took Duane a few weeks to recover from his adventure. There were bumps and bruises everywhere that needed to heal. During that time, Magic continued to drop in, boisterous and loud as always, never a mention of the

toboggan ride. Duane had already forgiven her. Duane's heart was incapable of holding a grudge. He would accept Magic for who she was, bossy yet playful, self-centered yet fun, but he would not forget who he was either. And he wouldn't forget how to say no.

9.
MAJOR PUFF FINDS A HOME
AND A HARE

THE STORY I AM about to tell you introduces a new soon-to-be friend of Duane's. But Duane is not in this story because Duane was not the first to meet her. It was Major Puff who had the honor. It happened in the spring.

Upon returning to the Very, Very Far North from his "migration" that was *not* at all a holiday, Major Puff was again in need of a home. Building it himself was not an option. A puffin who had descended from a long line of military heroes could not be expected to perform manual labor. Digging a burrow was naturally, and literally, beneath him. So the only remaining choice was to seize a home already dug.

This required time and effort. Let me remind you that Major Puff was a puffin whose ancestors were responsible for winning half a dozen wars, not to mention twenty-eighty significant battles and countless skirmishes of varied importance. Therefore, he had standards. Cleanliness was a priority, as was ample space for marching, which he practiced regularly and often. Also on the list—and quite frankly, at the top of the list—was abandonment. The burrow needed to be empty. Not to say that he wouldn't be willing to take a burrow by force if necessary, for the blood of conquerors flowed vigorously through his veins. But it seemed that in each and every case, the burrow most to his liking was one in which no one was currently living.

He marched from one spot to another, inspecting a burrow here and a burrow there, but none passed muster. He visited burrows he'd lived in from past years, but they looked worn and tired now; they lacked what Major Puff deemed "the proper puffin panache."

As the day drew closer to an end, he began to have doubts. He scolded himself for taking the migration that was in no way a vacation even though he didn't really have to migrate. Had he stayed the winter, he'd still have his old burrow. Had he stayed, that old burrow would have been kept clean and proper. At the very least, had he stayed, he'd still remember where he left it, which he now couldn't. Any lesser auk might have called it quits. Major Puff was *not* a lesser auk. He expanded his territory. He sharpened his senses. He remained alert.

At twilight's cusp, Major Puff believed he had at last found success. A burrow was situated in a beautiful meadow recently released from its snow covering. The door was simple but solidly built—an important consideration if and when under siege. So with chest puffed out and breath held in, he entered.

To his relief, nothing happened. He was not set upon by unreasonable hordes or ambushed by sneaky types. He wasn't compelled to offer stuttering apologies for trespassing or to make a hasty, panicked retreat in the heroic fashion of his parents, grandparents, and great-grandparents. The burrow, it seemed, was empty.

Even better, the burrow was very, very large.

Excellent, he thought to himself. *Plenty of room for marching in all directions. My skills will not be allowed to wither.*

One final test remained before Major Puff could give his stamp of approval. He spread a wing and allowed it to run along the floor. Inspecting his feather tips, he let out a contented sigh. "Not even a speck of dust," he said aloud.

"I should hope not. I've spent the better half of a day cleaning the place."

"Eeek!" replied Major Puff very loudly to the voice coming from the far corner of the room. It was the proper response, mind you, quite customary to the particular warrior clan to which Major Puff belonged. But the owner of the voice—a small, furry white hare with longish ears—didn't seem to care.

"Perhaps I cleaned too much. I worry about such things. What if I've made the place completely sterile? Shouldn't a home have a bit of bacteria lying about?"

Major Puff was truly bewildered. He stared

at the hare, who in turn stared back, apparently waiting for an answer.

"I . . . I . . . I do not know, madame," said Major Puff. "I err more toward cleanliness, I suppose."

His response seemed to satisfy the hare, who gave a series of quick, small nods, among an assortment of other twitches and jerks that never ceased. It looked as if she was in a constant state of noticing danger, then assessing the danger, and then finally dismissing the now *non*-danger to make way for a possibly worse danger about to strike. Major Puff found it exhausting just watching her.

"Agreed. Better safe than sorry. Look before you leap. A stitch in time, a bird in the hand, a sneeze in the wind, yes?"

"If you say so," offered Major Puff, having absolutely no idea what she was talking about.

It didn't matter. Disappointment set in for

Major Puff. He had no reason to continue the conversation. He took a final glance around the spacious, very clean, very secure burrow with a sad and heavy heart. It simply was not to his taste. And it had nothing to do with it already being inhabited by a very talkative hare. No, not at all. Major Puff would not hesitate to claim ownership if he really wanted the *almost* perfect burrow. He would not be afraid because a puffin of his lineage has no fear. So there was likely some other very good reason why he was leaving, but what that reason was, he couldn't presently say. He clicked his feet together, made a 180-degree turn, and began a slow march toward the door.

"Do you live near here?" the hare shouted after him. "I'm new to the area. Just arrived. Chose this spot. Thought it was least likely to bring calamity and destruction upon myself, but you never know for sure, do you?"

Major Puff wanted desperately to leave the burrow with the unpardonable yet invisible flaw as soon as possible. But he detected genuine worry in the hare's voice, so heroically, he turned 180 degrees again and addressed her. "It's quite safe, madame. I assure you," Major Puff said with authority. "Although I've just returned from my most recent migration, I've visited the area many times and never took issue."

The hare's ears perked up. "Oh my, you flew here? Oh my, oh my. *That* was very brave. Yes, very courageous. Couldn't see myself up in the sky."

For Major Puff to be told that he was brave and courageous was nothing new. He said as much to himself each and every day. But to hear those words come from someone else was an entirely exotic experience. He was caught off guard. "Oh, it's . . . it's no big deal," Major Puff replied.

The hare would hear none of it. "No big

deal? All that wind? All that rain? Not to mention the height. And you've done this more than once? My goodness, I've never been in the company of someone so brave."

"Really?" asked Major Puff, genuinely amazed. And then seizing the moment, he added, "Well, yes, I suppose one could see these trips as hazardous. The distance I cover is staggering. And I never know if a meal awaits me at the end of a long day of flapping, or if a hurricane might descend upon me without warning. There is risk. There is danger. But one does what one must."

Major Puff was delighted to find the hare listening with rapt attention. Her eyes were wide open and her front paws covered her mouth to muffle any cries of shock. Major Puff felt it was beyond flattering. It was as if he had walked into a surprise birthday party in his honor, or so he imagined, having never been given one.

"I should take my leave," he said gallantly, the sting of losing the burrow not so sharp now. He bowed his head.

"You could stay, you know."

Major Puff wasn't sure he heard correctly. "I beg your pardon?"

"Just saying. Lots of room. Very clean. Maybe too clean, but still. Comforting to have a brave soul about. I'd feel protected."

Major Puff's heart skipped a beat. There were rumblings in his chest area. A giggle escaped his beak, which made him blush. Having never experienced glee before, it threw Major Puff off-balance. But regaining self-control, he made it clear that he wasn't a puffin who compromised on discipline. "Let there be no mistake," Major Puff began. "*If* I stay, I will practice my marching every morning and sometimes at night as well."

"Well, that's a bonus for me, isn't it? I'm a hopper myself. Love to hop. Good for the circulation, so I'm told, in moderation. But marching would be a nice change of pace."

Another giggle escaped Major Puff's beak. Glee was turning into joy.

"I've set myself up in a room down that tunnel," the hare said, pointing, "but there are five other rooms to choose from down each of those tunnels."

"You dug all of this yourself, madame?"

The hare shrugged and smiled. "Nervous energy."

Major Puff paused. It was highly unusual for a puffin of his caliber to share his residence with a stranger. Yet aside from his military prowess, manners and charity were two other merits that defined his noble lineage. How could he evict this poor hare out into the elements, especially knowing that she built the burrow herself? No, Major Puff had to rise to the occasion. He had to break from tradition. "I accept your offer, madame, if the agreed terms are honored."

And they were. In fact, that very evening, after a celebratory cup of tea, Major Puff took up his marching practice around the burrow while the hare looked on in quiet yet twitchy awe.

10.
THE HARE GETS HER NAME, DUANE TAKES CHARGE, AND MAJOR PUFF HAS QUITE A DAY

S O IT WAS THAT Major Puff had made the hare's acquaintance first. Neither Duane, nor C.C., nor Handsome, nor Magic had yet laid eyes on her. And although Duane and Handsome met Major Puff back in the autumn, it was a brief meeting and, as you may recall, not altogether friendly.

Since then, Duane had been exploring more and more of the Very, Very Far North, including the other side of the river where Major Puff and the hare now shared a burrow. It was on one such walkabout that he crossed the hare's path. Let's begin this story just before that happened.

Duane strolled through a meadow made gloriously thick with grasses and wildflowers brightened by the springtime sun. The plants that he recognized, he named out loud in Latin, as C.C. had taught him from her books.

"Look! There's *Sacks of Frag and Spit on Toes*. Over here is a bunch of *Sacks of Frag Hop or Sit if Holy*."

Duane was of course pronouncing the names wrong because they were in Latin, and Latin is hard to pronounce. He should have said *Saxifraga cespitosa* and *Saxifraga oppositifolia*. But between you and me, don't you think it would be easier if he'd just said, "Look! There's a pretty white-and-yellow flower, and over here is a bunch of basically the same flower, only in purple"? Well,

I do. However, in the spirit of compromise, Duane will use common names of flowers, and I will add descriptions. So let's start again.

Duane strolled through a meadow made gloriously thick with grasses and wildflowers brightened by the springtime sun. The plants that he recognized, he named out loud, describing them as he saw fit.

"There are some white mountain avens," he said, pointing at flowers with eight creamy white petals surrounding a center of bright yellow filaments.

"There's a bunch of purple paintbrushes," he said, pointing at flowers that are pretty self-explanatory, I should think.

"And that is a field of cotton grass." Duane sighed, looking up a gentle slope densely dotted in puffs of white hair balls that swayed in the breeze.

Only, it was not cotton grass, or at least, not all of the white furry stuff was. Hopping up and down in one spot among the cotton grass was an equally white and furry creature. It was the arctic hare that currently shared a burrow with Major Puff.

"Twenty-eight," said the hare at the top of her twenty-eighth hop.

"Twenty-nine," she said, at the top of her next hop.

"Thirty," she said at—well, you get the picture.

Between hops thirty-one and forty-six, Duane paused to consider. He was reminded of his first encounter with Magic, another small white creature who appeared and disappeared right in front of him. But Magic was trying to trick him, which didn't seem the case with the hare currently hopping up and down. For one thing, she was staying in place and not moving about. For another, she hadn't yet seen Duane because she was facing another direction.

"Forty-seven," she announced at the top of her latest hop. She then spotted Duane as she was coming down, managing to get in an "Oh!" before disappearing beneath the grass. In a blink she was rising up again, continuing what she saying. This repeated over and over each time she was visible. It broke her sentences into small portions.

"I didn't see . . . you coming. Don't . . . mind me. I'm . . . just getting in . . . my daily deep . . . knee hops. I . . . try to do . . . a hundred. Good . . . for the circu— . . . lation, I am . . . told, just saying." All this she related cheerfully between hops forty-eight and fifty-eight.

Duane was delighted to have met someone new in the Very, Very Far North. He attempted a response between hops sixty-one and sixty-five but found that the hare's rising and falling was making conversation difficult. "Hello to y— . . . Ah, there you are! I was a— . . . What I meant to s— . . . Do you think you could . . . Oh my."

It didn't go as well as he had hoped.

Not willing to give up, Duane instead took a different approach. He crouched down in preparation, and then, from

hops seventy through seventy-six, he rose up in the air just as she did and landed at the same time too.

"Hello, my name is . . . Duane. I was won— . . . dering if you . . . might stop hop— . . . ping for a mo— . . . ment, please?"

That did the trick.

"Seventy-seven!" declared the hare, concluding her exercise. "Seventy-seven will do. Not a hundred, but no point in being a stickler, right? Said your name is Duane? Lovely to meet you, Duane. Don't have a name, personally. Wish I did. Can see the benefits of having a name. Getting one's attention at a distance. Personalizing a birthday cake and such. Major Puff calls me Madame. Very courteous, Major Puff. A real gentleman. Madame is nice. Not warm, though, as a name. Not familiar, if you get my meaning. Just saying. Are you two acquainted?"

"Am I—sorry, what?" Duane, who was already dizzy from the jumping, was now finding the hare's quick, clipped way of talking equally unbalancing, not to mention all the twitches and tics that accompanied her speech.

The hare had since moved on to leg stretches and alternate swivels at the waist. "Have you met Major Puff?" she asked.

In his head, Duane went through a list of everyone he'd encountered, which wasn't a long list. "The name sounds familiar, but I'm not completely sure. Could you describe him?"

"Black and white, orange beak, my size, more or less. Has wings—that's important. And a marcher. Ooh, yes, very serious about his marching. I'm taking lessons!" At which point the hare stopped her stretching and proceeded to march back and forth, with her very long back feet alternately thrusting high in the air.

"Oh yes, Major Puff." Duane nodded. Duane knew exactly who she meant because he now remembered the incident when Major Puff prevented Handsome from crossing the river. He told the whole story to the hare.

"So Major Puff thinks your friend is a great black-backed gull?"

"I'm afraid so."

"Ooh, that might explain the reluctance."

"The reluctance?" Duane asked.

The hare clarified while Duane concentrated very hard on understanding her clarification. "Doesn't get out much, the Major. Stays close to home. Poor dear. I suggested an outing once. 'Let's cross the river,' I said. 'Have a picnic, get some air.' Picnics are nice, don't you think? An excursion and a nibble? A break in the routine, just saying. Well, the Major was strongly against it. Concerned about traps and ambushes. Silly, really, having wings and all. Could fly over traps if he wanted. Still, not one to judge. Not one to throw carrots, lest you want carrots thrown at you, if you get my meaning."

Duane didn't get her meaning, or several of the other bits either, but he did get the gist of what she was saying, which was that Major Puff was not venturing far from their burrow because he was afraid of Handsome. Major Puff was still under the impression that Handsome was a great black-backed gull, which Handsome definitely was not. Therefore Major Puff was preventing himself from living his life based on a fear of an enemy he hadn't yet battled. From Duane's point of view, that was a shame. He thought that Handsome and Major Puff shared common qualities and might become good friends under the right circumstances.

"We need Major Puff to meet Handsome properly," said Duane. "He has to be convinced that Handsome is a musk ox."

"Ooh, could be a problem," said the hare, shaking her head. "If the Major has never met a musk ox while in sight of a great black-backed gull, he has nothing to compare, you see."

Duane nodded. The hare was right. As C.C. once explained, some facts need to be demonstrated in order to be believed. Thinking of C.C. gave Duane an idea.

"How does Major Puff feel about owls?" he asked as a plan started taking shape.

"Respects them, yes. No issue with owls as far as I know."

The next morning, Duane swam over to the Shipwreck to pay C.C. a visit. As usual, he found her in the windowed room at the back, conducting experiments for the advancement of knowledge toward the benefit of all.

"Do you have a picture of a great black-backed gull in one of your books, C.C.?"

"A great black-backed gull? Hmm." She thought and thought yet could not say for sure whether there was such a picture. Neither stymied nor frustrated, the owl's eyes grew a half size bigger and she let out a squeak of excitement. You see, it was a rare occasion when Duane came to her with a question that required research. C.C. *loved* research.

Methodically, she began leafing through the pages of her books. When one book had been scrutinized from front to back, Duane would remove it and set another one on the table in front of her. It took the whole morning until she could finally stop and say, "Aha!"

Duane stood beside her and looked down at

the spot she was pointing to on the page. "Is that a great black-backed gull?"

"It is indeed," said C.C. with a touch of pride.

"You're sure?" Duane asked.

C.C. studied Duane's face. Although she wasn't good with expressions and feelings, she had an inkling of a suspicion of a feeling that there was something more to Duane's request. "Why is it so important that I be sure that it's a great black-backed gull, Duane the polar bear?"

"Because I need you to dress up as one," Duane replied.

As you can imagine, an explanation was in order, and an explanation was given. Thereafter, Duane left the Shipwreck with two of C.C.'s books, having promised solemnly to take the most absolute best care of them so that they'd return to her in the exact same condition that they left.

* ❄ ❄ ❄ *

In the afternoon, Duane searched out his friend the arctic fox.

"Magic, I need you to help me play a trick."

"Yes!" Magic shouted with glee, not caring in the least what the trick was or upon whom it was to be played. "It's going to be great, Duane (*poke*)! The best, Duane (*poke*)! They will never see it coming, Duane (*poke*)!"

Magic's enthusiasm did not give Duane comfort. He realized that rules would need to be established from the start. He looked at Magic with the most serious expression he could produce. "No one is to be hurt or injured or even bruised."

"Huh?" said Magic, much less happily.

"No one is to be made to look foolish."

"Really?" asked Magic, slightly confused.

"And no one is to be made terribly scared, either."

"Oh, come on!" yelled Magic, throwing herself to the ground dramatically. "Not even scared? What's the point, then?"

Duane could see that he was losing Magic's interest, and in all honesty, he couldn't guarantee the last rule would be kept if his plan was to work. "Well, he might be scared," he began. "It's possible that he would be a little scared, or more than a little. In fact, it's possible he might become very scared at one or two moments. But in the long run, I think it will be for the benefit of all. Would you be willing to assist me?"

Magic was up on her paws in a second. "You had me at 'might be scared,' Duaney-Duane (*poke, poke*)!"

And with that, Duane explained to Magic what he had in mind and what he needed her to do.

In the evening, Duane met up with the hare back at the meadow to go over the details of the plan. "Tomorrow morning, come to the river's edge, where the stepping stones are," he instructed her.

"River's edge, stepping stones, understood. Which side?"

"Which side?" asked Duane.

"Of the river," the hare explained. "Remembered the story. Your friend—Handsome, was it?—didn't like the stones, crossing them and all. Made him dizzy. So best meet on your side, just saying. Not a fan of rivers myself. Strong currents, sneaky waterfalls, nasty ways to get hurt. But I won't object if it's for Major Puff. The greater good and such. A half dozen hops and it's done. So, tomorrow morning, river's edge, your side."

Duane marveled at how the hare recalled all the details of Handsome's river crossing and was willing to ignore her own fears in the assistance of Handsome and Major Puff. *She may jolt and jerk and speak in bits, but you can't say she isn't truly listening.*

As the hare turned to hop back to the burrow, Duane had an inspiration. It was risky, but Duane was in a risky frame of mind since taking charge of his plan. "How about Twitch?"

The hare turned around and tilted her head to one side.

"You told me yesterday that you wanted a name. Something personal? How about Twitch?"

The hare paused to think it through out loud. "Twitch is something I do. Won't deny that. Do other things too, mind—hop, bake, march. Wouldn't want to be called Hop. Or Bake. No ring to them to my ears. No music. And not right to be called March. Stepping on the Major's toes then, so to speak. Twitch is personable. Has humor in it. Could hear myself being called

Twitch. 'What's that you've got baking, Twitch?'
That sort of thing." The hare suddenly stopped.
She looked straight at Duane, as still and solid
as an iceberg, and he could feel her formidable
strength within the question she asked next.
"You're not laughing at me, are you?"

"Not at all. You said that you'd like a name
that was warm and personal. I'm laughing with
you, not at you, but only if you'd like that."

At first, the hare said nothing. Duane wondered if his risk-taking had gone too far. Until . . .

"Twitch it is, then." The hare nodded before
heading home. And Twitch it will be from here
on out.

Early the next morning, Duane awoke, ready to
put the plan into action. He ate a quick breakfast to fortify himself before venturing down
the hill to Handsome's field where the musk ox

stood sleeping next to the reflection pond.

"Handsome, come quick!" Duane yelled.

"Hmm? Wha—*snort!* Did someone . . . ? Duane, why are you here? I am confused." Poor Handsome. He'd been dreaming of a fancy ceremony for the Most Attractive Musk Ox Award, and just as he was about to receive the first place statuette, Duane came barging onstage.

Duane, of course, could not know that this was Handsome's dream, and even if he did, it would not matter. For Duane, it was best if Handsome was off-balance and not quite awake. "Handsome, there is a hare emergency that needs your attention!"

"What did you say? A hair emergency? Oh my, how horrible!"

I should explain to those of you who are presently being read to, rather than those of you reading this yourself, that Duane said "a hare"—H-A-R-E—"emergency," as in an urgent situation involving a rabbitlike creature such as Twitch. But Handsome thought that Duane said "a hair"—H-A-I-R—"emergency" that involved filaments such as fur or fuzz or wool or whatever grows off one's skin. Duane did not attempt to correct the misunderstanding because Duane knew how important grooming was to Handsome. If his friend should think that he was talking about a hair—H-A-I-R— situation, so be it, for it would generate the urgency needed to get to the next part of the plan.

Duane continued explaining with as much dramatic flair as he imagined Magic would use. "There's a creature, small and . . . and innocent! Her fur is—is—very soft and—and delicate!"

"Yes, go on," insisted Handsome, already caught up in the description.

"She's ensnared in a tangle of weeds. They're caught within her fur, and she cannot escape, Handsome!"

"Oh my," gasped the musk ox, in near shock. "The poor dear. The damage that those weeds must be doing to her follicles, I shudder to think."

"I wanted to help, Handsome. I wanted to free her of those terrible, thorny weeds! But I did not feel up to the task."

Handsome, now fully awake, addressed his friend in a most solemn tone of voice. "You did well to call upon me, Duane. No amateur should attempt a weed extraction. One wrong move and a patch of fur might be ripped straight out. Fetch my hairbrush; we must go to this poor creature's aid at once."

So focused was Handsome on the rescue mission that he didn't even hesitate as they neared the river, even though he had nothing but bad memories of the place. Was it a relief for him to find the creature in peril located on *his* side of the river? I cannot say for sure. He may very well have crossed the stepping stones anyway when the matter involved emergency grooming.

Prior to Handsome and Duane's arrival, Twitch had made her way across the river to place herself among a thicket of weeds. Just as planned, she made sure that the weeds wrapped around her legs and ears so that she looked completely trapped. When she caught sight of Duane and his musk ox companion, she declared aloud her woeful situation. "Help me! Trapped I am! Not comfortable, all brambly and such. Very scratchy. And prickly, too, just saying."

"Fear not, madame," said Handsome, coming quickly forward.

"Her name is Twitch, actually," Duane whispered.

"Ah. Well then, fear not, Twitch. I shall free you at once. It is a delicate operation. Try to stay calm and still and, well . . . less twitchy."

Handsome took the hairbrush from Duane and began to meticulously clear away the weeds from Twitch's fur. His concentration was impressive, as was his brushing skill.

Meanwhile, on the other side of the river, Magic had arrived just outside the burrow belonging to Major Puff and Twitch. Quietly, she cleared her throat and did a few limbering-up exercises in preparation for her task. She moved next to the burrow's door, took a deep breath, and let out a bone-chilling scream at the top of her lungs. Magic was so loud that she didn't hear the thump of Major Puff's head hitting the burrow ceiling when he jumped up in fright.

Magic then recited the speech she had prac-ticed with all the dramatic flair that Duane had attempted earlier. "Oh, who will save her? Who will save the defenseless arctic hare about to be attacked and perhaps eaten by that fiend?" Her performance was both powerful and convincing. Major Puff, who, after hearing the blood-curdling scream, thought he was under attack, had pushed up against the door to block any burrow breach. But as soon as he heard mention of an arctic hare, he rushed up and down all the burrow tunnels in search of Twitch, whom he of course could not find.

"My goodness," Major Puff fretted. "Madame is in peril."

He pulled open the burrow door and marched outside, where Magic was positioned with paw to forehead, mouth agape, trembling in fear, and wobbly. "Thank goodness someone has heard my cry!"

"Where is she? Where is Madame, and who

dares attack her?" demanded Major Puff.

"She is yonder, by the river's edge," replied Magic, a little too flowery in my opinion. "But what vile creature attacks her, I know not. It's large and horrible! Its back is black and . . . and . . . such claws! Who will save her?" Magic collapsed to the ground in a dead faint and tried not to giggle.

As for Major Puff, the description of Twitch's attacker was clearly understood. After his harrowing ordeal back in autumn, and after the necessary migration that was not in any way a holiday that followed, he returned to the Very, Very Far North realizing his enemy was still at large. Yes, he had made a friend in Twitch, but in the recent weeks, he hadn't strayed far from the burrow, fearing the unfinished war to come. In his own estimation, he had behaved cowardly. But not now. Now something was different. Major Puff's eyes narrowed in steely determination. "So we shall meet again, great black-backed gull. Attack Madame, will you? Not on my watch!"

In the recorded annals of puffin military campaigns, never did a puffin march into battle with such dignified grit. How his feet lifted in perfect form! The rhythm of his steps never faltered, never slowed. Major Puff almost pitied his enemy, who knew not what was coming. Marching across the meadow, down its gentle slope, leaving a swath of purple paintbrushes and cotton grass in his wake, he pushed toward the river. There, in the distance, Twitch lay on the far side, while just behind her loomed the great black-backed gull with one of its claws brushing down upon her back.

"Un-claw her!" Major Puff shouted across the river.

Handsome looked up from his brushing and weed-untangling, first in surprise and then in annoyance. "Oh, it's you again," Handsome said in a low, snooty voice. "I have no time for your nonsense. This poor creature is in trouble."

"Don't I know it! Lower your claw!"

"My what?" asked Handsome. "This? It's called a brush. At least that is what it is called by those of us who are civilized!"

The black-and-white puffin turned red in the face. "Your taunts do not hurt me! Let this battle begin!"

By this point, Twitch was feeling slightly guilty. She should have said something to calm Major Puff's nerves, but the truth was, all that brushing of her fur felt wonderful. It left her in a blissful daze and completely speechless. Major Puff interpreted her silence to mean she was perhaps near death. "I shall save you from this great black-backed gull, Madame!" he cried as he hopped across three river rocks.

"Again with the great black-backed gull? Do I have wings? How many times must I tell you that *I* am a musk ox?" Handsome shouted at the charging puffin. "If there is anyone likely to be a great black-backed gull, my guess is it's whatever that is!"

Handsome was now pointing up at the sky. Major Puff followed his direction and saw something that caused him much confusion, followed quickly by fear. Swooping down upon him with sharp talons thrusting out was a large bird covered mainly in white feathers except for its back, which was decidedly black. Its beak was long and yellow. Its eyes were small and beady. Immediately, the description of the puffin nation's most notorious enemy, as handed down from one puffin generation to the next, flooded Major Puff's memory. The thing flying above him did meet that description very well. So had he been wrong in assuming that the large creature now attacking Twitch was a great black-backed gull? Was that creature indeed a musk ox as it claimed, and was that in fact a brush it held and not a claw? Major Puff had to concede that it was, on both accounts. Under different circumstances, a puffin of his integrity would have immediately apologized to Handsome. This, however, had to be put off until later due to the actual great black-backed gull snatching him mid-flight and lifting him by its talons high into the air.

"Unhand me, dastardly villain!" Major Puff demanded. "Unhand me right now!"

These were brave words without a doubt, shouted up at an enemy much larger and much stronger. Yet even within the mighty clutch of the great black-backed gull's talons, which left him powerless as he was flown through the air, Major Puff couldn't help but notice that up close, his enemy looked much less impressive. For one thing, the black of its back was splotchy, as if its feathers had been painted. For another thing, its long yellow beak seemed to be attached to its head by a string that tied into a bow at the back. And as for the beady eyes, in truth, they looked like holes cut out of a mask. *I must be delirious*, Major Puff thought to himself. *All this excitement has left me dizzy. No matter. As long as Madame is safe.*

The chivalrous puffin lost himself in imagining his heroic death, unaware that the great black-backed gull had descended from the sky.

Its talons opened and Major Puff was released. He fell, but only briefly. The large open arms of Duane were there to receive him.

"Hello again, Major Puff," Duane said, smiling. Gently, he lowered the puffin to the ground. Already gathered in front of the polar bear and the puffin were Magic, Handsome, and Twitch. As you can imagine, here, too, an explanation was in order. To assist Duane

in explaining, he brought over the two books belonging to C.C. and turned to the pages that showed the illustrations and descriptions of both the great black-backed gull and the musk ox. From that point on, there was never any confusion in Major Puff's mind as to who was which. He turned to Handsome and apologized sincerely and humbly.

"Think nothing of it," replied Handsome, quite moved. "Your eloquent words prove you are a puffin of good breeding. I look forward to future conversations. Expect an invitation in the mail."

"Well, all's well that ends well." Twitch beamed. "The Major's got a friend, I've got a name, happy campers each and every, tickled pink, over the moon, five hops forward, no hops back, if you get my meaning."

No one did get Twitch's meaning exactly, but

they all understood that there was now a larger group of friends, which left everyone feeling a buzz of excitement for the possibilities that might follow. Twitch accompanied Major Puff back to the burrow, where a quiet cup of tea was in order after such a harrowing morning. Magic disappeared before anyone could notice. The excitement of playing a trick generated more energy than she knew what to do with. C.C. was back on the Shipwreck. She'd already removed the mask and untied the yellow beak that she'd made with paint and scrap pieces lying about. More challenging was scrubbing off the black paint that she'd applied to her back feathers. She would continue to wash until they were completely white again while she awaited the return of her two books.

As for Duane, he was carrying those books carefully while walking alongside Handsome, who required some more explanation.

"So you are telling me, Duane, that Twitch did not actually require emergency grooming?"

"No, Handsome, I confess that it was a trick."

"I am somewhat perturbed. Are we not friends? Why did you not simply ask me to join you at the river?"

"Would you have come to the river if I had asked?"

Handsome paused to consider. He had to concede that if asked, he would have most definitely said no. "Point taken, Duane. And when are you planning on telling the Major that the great black-backed gull is C.C.?"

"Soon," said Duane. "It seemed like a lot to throw at him all at once. And besides, he did act very heroically today. He should be allowed to have his moment."

"Agreed." Handsome nodded. "Etiquette demands such considerations."

The two friends parted company at Handsome's field. Before Duane could go home to his cave, he did have to return C.C.'s books in the exact same condition that they were in when he borrowed them, so it was better done sooner than later. As he walked down the sloping trail that led past the berry bushes and the tasty grasses and finally spilled out onto the Fabulous Beach, Duane had time to reflect on all that had happened. There were now two new friends in his life to get to know. His gift of Twitch's name was well received. He could see that Major Puff and Handsome would no longer be at odds. There was also a great story for all the friends to share with one another every now and again, each telling it from his or her point of view. Duane was proud of himself too.

He put together a complicated plan and was able to convince his friends to take part. He accomplished something for the benefit of others. It was a good day.

11.
DUANE MEETS A PAINTER
AND GETS SCARED

D URING THE SECOND SUMMER after Duane's
arrival in the Very, Very Far North, he
came across a ragged gray tent on the far side of
the river. It was pitched upon a cliff that looked
over the Cold, Cold Ocean. There were sturdy
wooden boxes near the tent; there was a small
rickety table and a chair; there was a lamp. But
much more interesting, there was a man, as well.

He was tall and thin, this man, with a

dollop of coarse white hair atop his head. He wore tweed pants with suspenders. He wore a long shirt with sleeves rolled up just below his elbows. Hanging from his mouth was a smoking pipe that curved off his bottom lip like the back of a snow goose. This man did not acknowledge Duane's arrival because he was facing the water, squinting in the sunlight.

Duane was curious. Why was he was looking at the Cold, Cold Ocean with such intensity? Duane turned to look at the ocean too, but all he saw was what he always saw: namely, the ocean. Duane tried looking harder. The results were no different. Duane was confused. You see, he didn't understand that the man was not just *looking* at the Cold, Cold Ocean but studying it, in all its rawness, unobstructed. Duane also didn't know that the contraption standing beside the man was an easel, and the square of white sitting upon it was an empty canvas. The man, you may have guessed, was a painter.

"Will you look at that," the man suddenly said.

Duane froze, uncertain whether the man was addressing him because he was still staring out at the water.

"I see midnight blue, persian blue, cornflower, powder, and sapphire. And whites?

There's porcelain, daisy, and pearl." The man took a puff of his pipe before turning toward Duane. "What do you see?"

"What do *I* see?" asked Duane quietly, realizing now that he was indeed being included in the conversation.

"Yes," said the man, with a sly smile. "What do you see out there, or over here, or anywhere around us? How does a polar bear such as yourself see this world?"

A polar bear such as myself, thought Duane, amused. He liked that expression. He began pointing in different directions as he spoke. "A polar bear such as myself sees tasty, juicy berries over there and delicious muffins over there."

"Muffins?" asked the man.

"Yes. That's where Twitch lives, and she is an excellent baker of muffins and other sweet goods. A polar bear such as myself likes eating tasty delicious things as often as I can."

"Is that it?" asked the man, frowning. "Are your eyes only in your stomach?"

Eyes in my stomach, considered Duane. *How odd an idea.* But he could see the man's point. If the world was nothing more than a map directing Duane to his next meal, then "eyes in his stomach" was an apt description. Duane considered the question further. What was the world to him? The world was big and mysterious. Duane, it seemed, learned one or two new things about the world every single day. Yet, the world also felt familiar, or if not familiar, then it felt right, as it should be. Even the surprises seemed as they should be. It was settled. Duane had an opinion. "A polar bear such as myself sees where he belongs."

"Go on," said the man, taking a puff from his pipe.

"I could, but it would be easier to explain during the winter," said Duane.

"Why the winter?"

"Because with the winter comes the snow and ice. I am much more in my element then, as C.C. would say. Will you be here in the winter?"

"I dare say no," said the man. "In winter, I would be very much out of my element here."

"That's a pity," Duane added with sincere sadness. "You will miss the best time of the year."

The man's attention was suddenly drawn back to the ocean. He rushed behind his easel. "Look at that light. If I don't get at it, I will miss the best time of the day as well."

Duane was intrigued. "What is it that you are going to do?"

"Capture that ocean and put it right here on this canvas," the man replied boldly, holding up the empty square of white.

Duane let out a laugh. It was not an impolite laugh because he genuinely thought the man was making a joke. "How silly!" said Duane, amused. "Imagine fitting the great big ocean into a little square."

The man was not offended by the laughter. In fact, he smiled at Duane and gave him a wink. "Yes, just imagine." Then he turned to his easel.

Duane watched him pick up a small, thin piece of wood and apply splotches of different colored goo along the border. Then he took a stick with bristles at one end and combined the colored goo together in the middle, creating new colors. Duane, led by his curiosity, stepped closer without even realizing it. He was mesmerized by what the man did next, which was to apply the colored goo onto the flat surface of the canvas. The man did it in long strokes and in dabs. He did it with thick lines and thin lines, lines fat with goo and lines that were mere shadows.

How curious, thought Duane, peering over the man's shoulder. Shapes were emerging now, and not only shapes, but movement. There were waves cutting in one direction and waves pushing over them. Waves, right there, where there was nothing before! Duane had never seen a painting before. He had never seen one being created. He looked at the ocean and then he looked at the canvas. Then he studied the ocean and he studied the canvas. Duane's jaw fell open. It was true. The man *was* capturing the ocean on the canvas. Duane looked out at the ocean for a third time, but now slightly to the left, and that was when Duane became very worried. Because in the direction he was now looking was the Shipwreck, and on the Shipwreck was C.C. If the man was capturing the ocean, then wouldn't it stand to reason that he would capture everything *in* the ocean too, including C.C.?

"How long does it usually take you to do your capturing?" Duane asked.

"I would guess a few hours, if I hurry."

Duane took little steps backward while he spoke. "Well, um, it was very nice to have met you, um, but I just remembered that I have to, um, what I mean is . . . bye." He quickly turned and ran in the direction of the Fabulous Beach. He had to warn C.C. to get off the Shipwreck as soon as possible before it was too late.

In order to get to the Fabulous Beach, Duane first had to swim across the river, but when he reached the riverbank, there was Major Puff practicing his summertime outdoor marching while Twitch was doing deep-knee hopping exercises to keep her circulation moving.

"Hello, Duane!" Twitch waved happily.

"Come join us for some exercise followed by crumpets."

"I can't, Twitch," said Duane. "I really can't."

The refusal of crumpets stopped Major Puff mid-march. Duane had never refused a crumpet since they'd met. This behavior was quite out of the ordinary. "Who are you?" Major Puff demanded, stepping in front of the polar bear. "And why are you disguised as Duane?"

"What? No, I am Duane!"

"A Duane who refuses crumpets?" asked Twitch. "Not likely. Not in a million years. Duane would never turn down one of my crumpets, or two, or five. Begs the question, doesn't it?"

"What question?"

"That if you are Duane, then it's possible that you've had a bout of amnesia and do not remember who you are or your true feelings about crumpets. Just saying."

"I repeat," growled Major Puff while peering suspiciously up at Duane, ready for beak-to-paw combat, "who are you?"

Duane glanced nervously in the direction of the Cold, Cold Ocean and saw something that made him grow frantic with fear. Coming in from the east was thick fog. It was shrouding everything in a mist as blank as the canvas that the man was painting on. *It's started*, Duane thought, completely misunderstanding what was happening. *The ocean is getting captured in the canvas and leaving nothing behind in return. Eventually it will reach the Shipwreck and swallow it up.*

Feeling slightly guilty for the insult he was about to commit, Duane simply stepped over Major Puff and ran directly into the river. "I'm sorry, but I can't stop to explain! C.C. is in danger and I must warn her!"

Duane splashed onto his belly and began

paddling across the river as fast as he could, leaving Twitch and Major Puff to stare at each other in confusion. When he reached the other side, he shook himself off. As exhausted as he felt, Duane pushed onward, up and over the river ridge and down the hilly path toward the Fabulous Beach. Coming up in the other direction were Handsome and Magic, apparently having an argument.

"There is absolutely no point in discussing this," Handsome was insisting impatiently. "It's like comparing snowballs to seaweed."

"Oh, come on!" Magic responded, while falling dramatically on her back in utter disbelief. "It's so obvious! You'd have to have your head stuck in an unlit fox hole not to see the difference."

"That would be the most unlikely place I should choose to place my head. But even if I did, my opinion would remain steadfast."

At this point, Magic spotted Duane rushing down the hilly path toward them. "Just the polar bear we need right now!" she shouted happily, jumping back on her feet. "We have a question, Duane."

"No time to talk! No time to talk!" replied Duane, not stopping or even slowing.

"It will just take a second. Musk ox fur or fox fur—which is softer?"

"I don't know," Duane gasped while trying to squeeze past the two of them.

"Oh, come on!" insisted Magic. "It's a simple question. Just tell Handsome that my fur is way softer than his."

"I don't know! I don't care!" yelled Duane, causing both Handsome and Magic to raise an eyebrow. "C.C. is in danger of getting captured and I must warn her!"

Handsome and Magic watched as Duane continued to run down the hilly path toward the Fabulous Beach. By the time he disappeared behind a corner, Handsome looked at Magic and sniffed. "Well, obviously he was agreeing with my position."

Meanwhile, Duane rushed through the grassy meadows and around the berry bushes and onto the Fabulous Beach in time to see the ocean fog moving ever closer to the Shipwreck. *Oh dear*, he

thought. *The man is working very quickly. The Cold, Cold Ocean will be completely gone soon.*

Without stopping to catch his breath, Duane leaped into what was left of the Cold, Cold Ocean and paddled toward the Shipwreck. As he neared C.C.'s home, so too did the fog, coming from the other direction. From Duane's

perspective, it was as if a giant hand was thrusting out of the sky and stealing bits of the world he knew and cherished. And it occurred to Duane that if his effort was in vain, if he reached C.C. but not in time to get her away, then he would also be captured in the canvas. It was a frightening thought. *But at least C.C. won't be alone. We will be captured together. We'll share memories of the Very, Very Far North to pass the time.*

Duane swam through the gash in the bow of the Shipwreck. "C.C.!" he cried. "C.C., where are you?"

Duane ran up the rickety stairway and down the long corridor. "C.C.! We must get away or risk being captured!"

Duane reached the end of the corridor and pushed open the door to C.C.'s room, where C.C. herself was perched on the table, staring at Duane with annoyance. "I thought we agreed on knocking first before entering, Duane the polar bear."

"I remembered that, C.C.; I remembered about the knocking before entering, and I apologize for not doing so, but it is terribly urgent!" gasped Duane, placing a paw onto the table to steady himself as he caught his breath.

"That is what I gather. Please inform me of what is so urgent."

Instead of explaining, Duane became eerily silent because directly behind C.C. was the wall of windows, and Duane could see the white fog moving in. Within seconds, it had covered up the entire view of the ocean. "It's too late, C.C.," Duane whispered. "I'm too late." His heart filled with the deepest sadness he had ever known. "I'm so sorry. I tried, but I failed. You've been such a good friend, C.C., but I wasn't a good friend back." And then Duane lifted his paws to his eyes and cried as pitifully as any polar bear has ever cried. "Boo-hoo-hoo!"

C.C., for her part, had not a clue what was going on. It was enough for her to keep up with Duane's different emotions, studying them, naming them, and thinking about the proper way to respond to them. But on top of all that, she was trying to figure out what on earth he was so upset about. "Duane the polar bear, did you say something about being captured?"

Duane kept his paws overs his eyes while he continued to cry. "Yes, boo-hoo-hoo!"

"Who is capturing us?"

"The man, boo-hoo-hoo!"

"Which man are you referring to?"

"The one with the blank square and the hairy stick and all the colored goo, boo-hoo-hoo!"

I think this is an opportune time to acknowledge just how smart C.C. the snowy owl is. Had someone come up to you, blubbering about being captured by a man with a blank square and hairy stick and "all the colored goo," you— or I, for that matter—would back away as fast as possible. But C.C. did not flinch, other than to tilt her head slightly to the side as she worked through all those cryptic clues. "Are you talking about a painter?"

Duane stopped crying. "Huh?" he asked, paws still covering his eyes.

"Come and look at this," said C.C., returning to her large, heavy book and flipping through the pages with her wing.

Duane lowered his paws just enough for his wet, red eyes to peer over them and see what C.C. was doing. He sniffed. Then, because he was a polar bear of a curious nature, he moved over to where the owl was, despite the great sadness he still felt.

"Aha," said C.C. pointing to the page beneath her. "Is this what you were talking about?"

There on the page was a drawing of a person standing at an easel and painting. It was not the same person as the man that Duane encountered, but Duane made the connection nonetheless. C.C. went on to explain that a painter didn't actually capture the things being painted. That man may have been depicting the ocean on his blank square, but that didn't mean it would affect the real ocean. To Duane's great relief, this fact was confirmed when he looked up and saw through the wall of windows that the fog had lifted and the Cold, Cold Ocean was once again where it should be.

"So these pictures in your books were not always there? They were drawn by someone too?" Duane asked.

"Yes."

"And the real things *didn't* disappear after they were drawn."

"Without a doubt," replied C.C.

Duane let out a big sigh. "*Phew*. There are a lot of pictures in your books, including one of a polar bear. It scares me to consider what might have gone missing."

With a much lighter heart, Duane took leave of C.C., making sure to close the door behind him. He swam back to land and walked up the hilly path to his cave, doing both at a leisurely pace. Although he was ready to call it a day after so much excitement and emotion, it suddenly occurred to Duane that he never saw the finished painting. So he turned in the direction of the man's camping spot and made his way.

Upon reaching the far side of the river, there was Twitch and Major Puff, as well as Handsome and Magic in deep discussion. Spotting Duane, they immediately came forward.

"Your behavior earlier was less than exemplary," Handsome scolded. "We believe an explanation is in order."

"That is, if you actually are Duane and not a great black-backed gull in disguise, as Major Puff believes," Twitch added.

Duane apologized to his friends and then proceeded to explain about the painter and his painting and what Duane thought was happening and then what was actually happening and that C.C. was completely safe the whole time.

"Oh my goodness, Duane!" exclaimed Magic, rolling her eyes very dramatically. "I can't believe you thought that the ocean was going to disappear. I mean—really! How could you be so naive?" Magic was feeling quite superior at that moment, but I will tell you now that in truth, while Duane was relaying his story, she took three or more worried glances toward the ocean, making sure it was still there.

"I'm going to go over and see the finished painting now," said Duane. "You are all welcome to join me."

Curious about this painting and this stranger who made it, his friends did join him. But when they arrived at the cliff's edge, the painting had not been completed. "The fog suddenly came in out of nowhere and blocked my view," the man explained.

Duane smiled at this news. "As it should be," he said, more to himself than to anyone else.

"I'll have to try again tomorrow. In the meantime, I can show you my other work, if you'd like."

The man opened one of his wooden crates and pulled out a half dozen paintings. There was one showing the river in the late evening, with a few stars twinkling in the purple sky. There was one showing the hills where Duane's cave was, with a morning light washing them in an all too familiar golden hue. As the man displayed the paintings, Twitch made small comments.

"Ooh, yes." She nodded. "That's a good likeness. Ooh, and look, there's our burrow, Major Puff! Very romantic setting, don't you think? Just saying."

After the viewing, thank-yous and goodbyes were exchanged. And just before Duane took leave, the man asked him, "Do you think that a polar bear such as yourself, and your friends, would mind if I came up here each summer to paint?"

"I shouldn't think it a problem," Duane answered. But then he hesitated because, as confident as he was that he understood C.C.'s explanation and felt assured that nothing would disappear in the process of painting, he wondered if there were other outcomes he should be concerned about. So he added, "As long as you leave the Cold, Cold Ocean where it is, after you've painted it, and you don't move any of the mountains around or reshuffle the hills so that I can't find my cave anymore. A polar bear such as myself likes to know where his home is."

The man agreed, promising to leave everything how he found it.

Several weeks later, while Duane was on a walkabout, he met Sun Girl and the Pack in a stretch of flat, empty land. They stopped in the middle of the flat, empty land to chat. In their conversation, Duane told them about the man and his paintings. He described each one to the best of his memory. As he was doing so, Duane realized that he wasn't as impressed with them as he was at first. "Something was missing from the pictures," he tried to explain.

Sun Girl nodded in understanding. "*You* were missing. And your friends. And me."

"And us," the Pack added.

Duane knew that Sun Girl was right. The paintings showed the Very, Very Far North but no one within it. "Do you think he forgot to put us in?"

Sun Girl shrugged. "In any case, he should come here in the winter to make his pictures. We're much more in our element then."

About that, too, Duane knew Sun Girl was right.

12.
ANOTHER FRIEND

I N THE COURSE OF the tales told so far, Duane had met and befriended C.C., Handsome, Magic, Twitch, Major Puff, Sun Girl, and the Pack. But there is one other character not yet present. Her name would eventually be Boo, and this story is her introduction.

The exact date of when Boo came into the Very, Very Far North remains a mystery. There was a time when she was not around, and there was a time when she was around, but at what moment that happened is something neither Duane nor anyone else could explain.

Technically, Duane had made her acquaintance first, which was peculiar, given that Boo had already been in the company of Handsome for quite a while. A musk ox less preoccupied with his reflection might have noticed, but it wasn't until after Duane dropped by Handsome's meadow and said, "Hello. And who might you be?" that Handsome became aware that for all that time, he'd been speaking to a stranger.

"What do you mean, 'And who might you be?'" he demanded of Duane. "I hope you haven't gone and bumped your head and forgotten everything."

"No, I—" Duane was about to explain before being cut off.

"Good. Memory loss is a tedious affair. It

requires repeating bits of information that are inconsequential and boring, like how one musk ox is the third cousin once removed of another musk ox on its mother's side. If our every social occasion means another explanation of how you, Duane, and I are well acquainted, then I foresee many headaches in my future."

"I wasn't addressing you, Handsome," Duane finally got in. "I was addressing her."

"Her?" asked Handsome, genuinely surprised. He raised and turned his head, but by then, all he could see was a flash of light brown fur as the "her" in question darted around a far hill. "Do you mean to tell me that for the past some odd days, it wasn't you with whom I was discussing grooming tips?"

"Sadly, that wasn't I," said Duane, although secretly, he wasn't that sad.

"Well, I suppose I should be upset by the

intrusion. Then again, it didn't feel much like an intrusion. I simply talked and the stranger listened. An ideal arrangement, in my books."

Duane could have pointed out to Handsome how very *not* ideal an arrangement that might be for some. But that would have required explaining to him that others also have things to say and share about their lives. Like family genealogy, such an explanation would fall under Handsome's Inconsequential and Boring Bits category. Handsome would have been distracted by his hand mirror long before Duane talked about the merits of listening and paying attention to whom you are addressing.

A better use of his time was to share his discovery of the stranger to his other friends, which he did right away.

"Describe what she looks like?" asked C.C. back on the Shipwreck.

"She looks like Handsome," said Duane, who then hesitated. "But not really."

"She is, but she isn't?"

"Yes." Duane nodded. He could tell by C.C.'s expression that he was doing a poor job of description-giving so far. "She's smaller than Handsome, but bigger than you. And Twitch. And Major Puff. And Magic."

"Fur or feathers?"

"Pardon me?" asked Duane, confused.

"Is the stranger covered in fur or feathers?"

"Ah. Fur, I believe."

"So no wings," said C.C. with a curt nod. "Two legs or four legs?"

"Four," said Duane confidently. He grinned, as he was now getting the hang of description-giving. "Four legs *and* four hooves," he added knowingly.

"Obviously," said C.C. "Any markings? Anything unusual that would allow me to compare her description to the ones in my book?"

Duane paused to think. It was a long pause, to be honest. A very, *very* long pause. His eyes suddenly brightened. "Well, she had . . ."

"Yes?" C.C. encouraged.

"On her head, she had . . ."

"Yes, yes, go on," C.C. prodded.

"Trees."

"Trees?"

"Yes, trees." Duane nodded.

"You're telling me that she had several trees on her head?"

"Two trees, to be exact."

C.C. stared at Duane in a way that made him feel that description-giving was a skill he could not possibly be worse at. As he himself considered the unlikelihood that the stranger would have trees growing out of her head, his eyes brightened again. "Not trees. Tree branches."

"She had branches growing on her head?"

"Yes?" said Duane meekly, worried that he was about to get another harsh stare.

"Well, why didn't you say so?" shouted C.C. happily.

"I thought I did."

"They're not tree branches, Duane—they're antlers," she explained while she flipped through the pages of one of her large books. "Which means that the stranger is probably a caribou."

C.C. pointed her wing at a drawing. Duane peered down at it. "Yes, that's her! That's the stranger! Although she's not a stranger now that we know what she is."

That wasn't completely true, as Duane later found out when he told Twitch and Major Puff. Knowing what the stranger looked like didn't explain what the stranger was like in personality and temperament.

"Is she dangerous?" asked Twitch. "Snarling teeth and all? Ooh, I wouldn't like that, not one bit."

"I didn't see any snarling teeth," said Duane.

"Vicious claws, maybe? Razor-sharp weapons slashing about? Just the sound of them cutting through the air gives me chills."

"I didn't see any claws, either," said Duane.

"But what about those antlers?" Twitch went on. "Getting stabbed or gored on the pointy ends?

That sounds like nasty business, to be sure."

Major Puff saw an opportunity to step in and be brave. "Have no fear, Madame. I would not let such a creature harm a single hair on your body. I would march circles around her, creating a swirl of confusion on the battlefield!"

"She's quite fast," said Duane, remembering how quickly the caribou ran off.

"Posh and twaddle and fiddlesticks!" shouted Major Puff, as if by saying those words he countered the fact of the caribou's quickness.

"The stranger was in the company of Handsome for quite a while, and at no time did Handsome ever feel threatened or in danger," Duane pointed out.

Major Puff would have none of it. "That's exactly what the cunning stranger hoped to achieve. By lulling our musk ox ally into a false sense of security, she has his defenses down so she can spring upon him in a sneak attack and then run away. Classic puffin military tactics!"

Duane remained doubtful. "When I tried to say hello, she looked truly alarmed. There was no snarling or slashing or stabbing. But there was fear in her eyes. I think she's shy."

Twitch's heart melted immediately. "Oh, the poor thing. What she needs is a warm cup of tea and some of my shortbread cookies and no personal questions. Talk about the weather. *A bit chilly today, yes? Looks like a snowstorm is on its way, don't you think?* Nothing wrong with weather conversation. Weather talk gets short shrift in my opinion. But no one gets offended during weather chats and no one is made to blush. Just saying."

Even though the stranger could now be identified in looks and temperament, Duane was not sure how to go about meeting her again, which he felt was important and necessary. Repeating his first attempt by just coming up to her and saying hello didn't seem wise. She'd likely run off again. Since Magic was amazing when it came to making unexpected entrances and exits, he decided to consult her.

"Oh, Duane, Duane, Duane (*poke, poke, poke*)!" exclaimed Magic in her typically over-dramatic fashion. Duane remained silent until the scolding part of the conversation was over and the problem-solving part could begin. "You cannot just walk up to a caribou, all jolly and loud and how-do-you-do! You might as well greet Twitch with a well-thrown snowball—"

"I would never do that," Duane interrupted, despite his intention to remain silent.

"Of course you wouldn't, Duane (*poke*). *That's* my point! Would you take Handsome's hair-brush when he wasn't looking and dip it in purple paint?"

"What? No! That's a horrible thought." Duane was shocked.

"Of course it is, Duane (*poke*)! *That's* my point! Would you sneak up behind C.C. wearing a skeleton mask?"

"No, I would never do that!" Duane protested, unable to contain himself. "Wait a minute—didn't you sneak up behind C.C. wearing a skeleton mask last Tuesday, Magic?"

"Yes! That's my point. That's exactly the point I'm trying to make!"

"So you're saying . . ." Duane stopped talking, yet his mouth remained open. He had absolutely no idea what point Magic was making. "I must confess that I'm confused."

Magic gave a loud and dramatic sigh. "Duane, if you want to meet the shy stranger, then don't."

"Don't meet the stranger?"

"Yes, don't, and eventually it will all work out."

"But . . . but . . . but how does that work, exactly?" As usual, Magic had already disappeared into one of the many holes leading to her den.

The next day, as Duane headed out of his cave and down the hill, he spotted the stranger grazing near Handsome. Duane decided to take Magic's advice, at least to the extent that he understood it. As he approached nearer, he could hear Handsome going on about something.

"It's always one hundred brush strokes on the right flank and then another hundred brush strokes on the left, once a day, every day. I cannot stress the importance of consistency when it comes to fur maintenance."

"Hello, Handsome," said Duane.

"Oh, hello, Duane. We've just been discussing a proper brushing regimen for keeping one's fur lustrous."

"Have you, now?" Duane replied, neither addressing the caribou nor even looking in her direction. As he continued his conversation with Handsome, it was clear that the stranger was content to graze nearby, listening. On a few occasions Duane noticed her nod her head in agreement with a comment.

Over the course of the week, all the other friends dropped by Handsome's field to chat, without ever putting the uncomfortable spotlight on the caribou, yet at the same time, never excluding her from the conversation. But on the day when Twitch stopped in with a batch of shortbread cookies after everyone else had already arrived, something small but significant happened.

"Oooh, I don't like the look of those clouds," said Twitch, glancing up at the sky. "All dark and menacing, they are. Thunderclouds, if you ask me. We're in for a thunderstorm; mark my words."

"I don't like thunder. It scares me," said the caribou in a voice that was barely audible.

"What was that, eh?" asked Major Puff.

"She doesn't like thunder," repeated Twitch, whose long ears were excellent for hearing the caribou's comment. "Nor do I, dear, nor do I," Twitch agreed.

Magic, C.C., and Handsome had been involved in their own conversation at the time and missed what had happened.

"Nor do you what, Twitch?" asked C.C.

But before she could answer, Duane, who was quietly observing everybody, spoke up. "You see, Twitch was commenting on the weather,

and how it was likely that a thunderstorm may come, and Boo then remarked that she did not like thunder."

It was the first time Duane tried out the name, although he'd already given it some serious thought. This time all the friends did look toward the stranger, wondering how she'd respond. There was a tense moment as she felt all eyes upon her, but it was a moment softened by the smiles and good intentions that came with them. Boo smiled back, ever so briefly;

she approved of her name, and the others were content in knowing their circle of friends had grown by one.

"Would you like to hear a joke?" asked C.C. to the group, pulling the focus away from Boo.

"Yes, but from Duane," insisted Handsome. "Your jokes require lengthy understanding of the topic it's based on, which is quite taxing, I find."

"Oh, Handsome, shush now!" said Twitch.

And so continued the lively conversation that now included Boo.

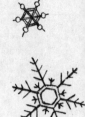

13.
PAINTING AN ICEBERG

WE ARE NEARING THE end of this book. I, as your narrator, am already feeling the coming separation when we will part company. There is a sadness, I confess.

It reminds me of an occasion when Duane dropped by on Squint during one of the painter's annual summer visits. Squint is the painter that we'd met earlier. It's likely that he had another name prior to coming up to the Very,

Very Far North, but Squint is the name Duane gave him, so Squint he will be.

Squint was sitting on his stool at the cliffside above the Cold, Cold Ocean, facing the empty square on his easel, and there was an iceberg behind it, far in the distance.

Duane stood behind Squint and watched him paint. He tried to be quiet. He tried to be respectful. He tried to be thoughtful. He stroked his chin, as he'd seen C.C. do with one of her wings when she was thinking. He nodded

approvingly, as he'd seen Handsome do on occa-sion, but Duane wasn't quite sure what he was approving of.

"You're painting that iceberg," Duane observed out loud.

"Yes, I am," replied Squint.

"Hmm, I see," said Duane, nodding *purpose-fully* this time.

In the pause that followed, Duane realized that he didn't see at all. "Why?" he asked.

"Why what, Duane?"

"Why are you painting that iceberg?"

"It's beautiful when it sparkles in the sun-light," replied Squint.

This was something Duane wholeheartedly agreed with, as ice was at the top of his list of wonderful, beautiful things in the world. This would have also been an ideal moment to nod *agreeably*. But the moment passed too soon.

In the next moment, Duane had reached a conclusion. "And so you paint beautiful things?" he asked Squint.

"I paint sad things too. And scary things and lonely things."

Beautiful things, sad things, scary things, and lonely things, thought Duane. This was a description of a single day in his life. Painting it all seemed like a lot of work. "Why don't you just *look* at the iceberg?"

"All right," said Squint. He put down his brush and stood beside Duane. Together they looked at the beautiful, sparkly iceberg.

In the next moment, the sun rose higher. Its rays passed above the clouds, and the clouds, in turn, brushed shadows onto the sleek surfaces of the iceberg and the surrounding water.

"Eventually, it will melt," said Squint matter-of-factly.

To Duane, a melted iceberg would unquestionably fall under the Sad Things category. "It will end up a puddle," Duane said.

"Lost in an ocean," added Squint.

Duane scratched his neck, just below his jaw. "Would you paint a puddle lost in an ocean?"

"Not today," said Squint. "Today is a day to paint icebergs." Then he sat back on his stool.

Duane continued to stand and stare at the beautiful, sparkly ice. He found himself nodding before he even realized he was doing it. This time he was nodding *knowingly*. "If you capture the iceberg on the square," he began, "then it will stay the same forever and ever?"

"In a way, yes," replied Squint.

Duane sighed. It was a small sigh stuffed with lots of feelings. *An iceberg preserved in time.* He was sure that his grandfather clock with the missing hands would have something to say on the topic. "I should let you get on with it, then."

14.
ONE FINAL STORY

THERE HAS BEEN SOME discussion among the characters. The question came up of how to bring this book to a proper ending. C.C. thought it best to show you a map, along with clear instructions on how to find the Very, Very Far North. Handsome was sure you'd want a list of his grooming tips. Magic thought it would be a great trick to reprint the same stories over and over again so that you stayed up all night reading them until you finally figured out something was wrong, but by then it would be morning and you would be too tired to go to school. Major Puff insisted that a complete history of all the puffin wars would fit in perfectly. Boo then said, "It would make the book too long." Nobody heard her except Twitch, but she didn't want to repeat what Boo said so as not to hurt the Major's feelings. Duane said that I should end the book with something that is fun, that takes place in winter, and that involves a bit of adventure, but nothing too scary.

Well, that started a whole new discussion. Many stories were suggested, but this is what the characters agreed upon:

Duane awoke from a refreshing nap with more energy than he knew what to do with.

When he tried to sit still, his left foot tapped. When he focused on keeping his left foot still, his claws twiddled. When he concentrated on keeping his claws still, his right foot began to shake. So he left his cave and walked over to the frozen river, because a day when you have more energy than you know what to do with is a day when you should be practicing your sliding.

It had been Duane's goal for a long time to be able to reach the other side of the river with a single slide. Standing at the riverbank, he felt confident that this would be the day. The conditions were perfect. The river ice was smooth, and what little wind Duane detected was blowing from behind. "Plus, I have more energy than I know what to do with," he said to himself.

For this historic attempt, a running start was necessary. Duane would need to pick up as much speed as possible. He walked back from the smooth ice, up the riverbank side, counting fifty steps out loud as he went along. "One, two, three, four . . ." But when he got to steps thirty-seven and higher, he lost interest in counting numbers and started thinking of other things to count, like Snow Delight flavors. "Thirty-eight, thirty-nine, blackberry, huckleberry, forty-five, strawberry, thirty-two, raspberry . . ." So it is very likely that he took fewer than fifty steps, or perhaps many more.

In any case, Duane eventually stopped and turned to face the frozen river. If he made it across to the other side, he would have an amazing story to tell his friends later. He could well imagine their expressions of awe and their demands that he tell the story again. There might be an impromptu celebration including Snow Delights of different flavors, all raised in a toast to Duane's accomplishment. Unless they didn't believe him. Unless they thought he was exaggerating. Unless they demanded proof. Then he would have to slide again with everyone watching so that there would be witnesses.

But what if he didn't have as much energy for that attempt? What if he was slightly tuckered out from the first attempt or from eating several delicious blackberry Snow Delights? What if he didn't slide completely across the river the second time? His friends would think he'd lied, even though he absolutely did make it across the first time. Why even bother trying the first time if everyone was going to call him a liar later? Duane was offended that his friends wouldn't give him the benefit of the doubt. True friends should believe one another, he insisted, and he was about to say just that when he remembered that his friends weren't there. "This whole conversation has been happening in my head," he scolded himself. "And I still don't even know if I *can* make it across the river yet."

With a shrug, Duane took off down the

riverbank, going as fast as his legs would carry him. *Whoosh!* went the air rushing to get out of his way. Duane felt unstoppable. As he reached the frozen shore, he lunged forward headfirst, his belly making slippery contact with the flat, smooth ice. *Whoosh!* went the air again. Duane slid at a stupendous speed. It was amazing. It felt as if he hadn't yet slowed down at all. In seconds he had already crossed a quarter of the way. "At this rate, I will make it across to the other side for sure."

Duane's attention was drawn to a figure coming toward him along the frozen ice. It was Sun Girl. Duane knew it was Sun Girl because she was wearing the bright red parka she loved so much. *What a relief*, thought Duane, *for now I will have a witness to my record-breaking slide so I won't have to do it again later to prove to my friends that I did it a first time.*

"Sun Girl!" Duane yelled. "Look at me! I'm about to make history!"

If Sun Girl yelled anything back, Duane was still too far away to hear it, but she did wave in greeting. "If she waved, that means she saw me. And if she then sees me reach the other side, my friends will have to believe me and hold a party in my honor, and I will eat lots of delicious Snow Delights." Even at the speed he was sliding across

the ice, Duane could still take the time to imagine how delicious one or four blackberry Snow Delights would taste.

"Although, I wonder," Duane hesitated, "if Sun Girl was really saying hello. Waving both arms frantically doesn't really seem like a proper hello greeting. It seems more of a wave one would give if you were trying to warn someone of something."

And that was when Duane noticed a large round hole cut in the river ice, directly in the path he was sliding along. "Definitely a warning wave," Duane concluded.

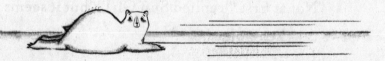

With great effort, he attempted to stop his slide, first by using his front paws, then by using his back paws, then by using all paws, and then by trying to flip himself onto his back. All he managed to do was rotate 180 degrees so that he was sliding tailfirst instead of headfirst, which still had its merits, because when he finally did slide directly into the ice hole, he found himself stuck snugly in the river from the waist down, which is much better than being stuck the other way, from the waist up.

"Hello, Duane," said Sun Girl when she reached him. "I see you've found my fishing hole."

"I did," Duane agreed. "Were you having much success?"

"Not at first," replied Sun Girl, "but it seems I've caught a polar bear."

"Yes, that would be me."

"Will you be there long, Duane?" asked Sun Girl. "I did have my heart set on a fish dinner tonight."

"I completely understand. And I shouldn't be more than two shakes of a paw." Duane pushed his front paws down against the ice in an effort to lift himself out of the hole. Even with having more energy than he knew what to do with, he didn't have much success. "Maybe four shakes of a paw," he clarified. Again he tried, but the results were no different.

"I was wondering," Duane began, "perhaps you could encourage larger fish to come by if you cut your fishing hole a little bit wider?"

"I would do that, except my ice saw went into the water along with my fishing spear when you slid into the hole."

"Oh," said Duane, discouraged. "In that case, would you ask some of my friends to come

and help? I'm quite wedged in here, and my bottom is getting very, very wet."

Sun Girl agreed, and while she went off in search of assistance, Duane continued staying wedged in the fishing hole, pondering how the day was turning out quite differently from how he had imagined. There would be no historical single slide across the river, no amazing story to tell, and no impromptu celebration complete with blackberry Snow Delights. "You can't plan these things," he told himself. "You can have hopes and you can have goals, but a day will take you where a day wants to go."

Eventually, Sun Girl returned with Handsome, Boo, Major Puff, Twitch, and Magic, as well as her eight sled dogs who referred to themselves as the Pack. She tied one end of a rope around Duane's waist and then wrapped the remaining length around everyone else except Major Puff, who felt he would be more useful giving commands.

"Heave!" shouted the Major.

The team of friends did heave, and the ice around Duane began to crack.

"Heave!" shouted the Major, this time with even more vigor. "Come on; put some muscle into it!"

The fishing hole's edge started to crumble.

"Heave!" shouted the Major, who was quite enjoying himself. "We're nearly there, lads!"

With a definitive pop, Duane was set free, sending the team of friends onto their backsides. Only seconds later, C.C. flew in to join the group. She'd been following Duane's ordeal through her telescope back on the Shipwreck and rushed over as soon as she could with a small jar of grease. Sadly, her arrival was too late to apply some science to the situation.

Duane stood up and shook himself off. Together with Sun Girl, he inspected the fishing hole, which now looked much less round. "I seem to have broken it," he said apologetically.

Sun Girl nodded in agreement.

Duane felt personally responsible, so he crouched beside the hole and thrust one paw into the water. He thrashed about for a few seconds and shortly after, the ice saw and spear bobbed up to the surface. Sun Girl was grateful.

"Come on, Duane!" demanded Magic. "We are all dying to know how you became wedged in the fishing hole!"

"No doubt, there is an amusing story worth telling, yes?" asked Handsome.

"As a matter of fact, there is," began Duane. "You see, I woke up from a nap with more energy than I knew what to do with, so I—"

Twitch interrupted. "I would like to suggest that we continue hearing the story at my and Major Puff's residence. We will be serving tea, and berries that I've saved from last summer. Snow Delights are optional for those who prefer them."

The present company, including Sun Girl and the Pack, approved of this suggestion, allowing the Major to take the lead. "This way, lads!"

Duane held back until everyone had gone up ahead. He looked one last time at the broken fishing hole that had prevented him from making history. But he grinned a very big grin anyway, because in a short while, he would be encircled by his friends, telling them an interesting story and eating blackberry Snow Delights. "Sometimes a day has a change of heart and decides to take you where *you* want to go."

IN CONCLUSION

W E HAVE REACHED THE point in the book where we must part company. I have no doubt that there will be more stories to tell, but what happens tomorrow or the day after, I cannot say for sure. Whether Duane feels an itch to explore or a stronger pull to sleep in until noon is anyone's guess. It's conceivable that Twitch will want to do some baking in the morning, but she might not. She may choose to join Major Puff in some early marching drills. It's likely that C.C. will be working on an experiment toward the benefit of all, but she may decide that a day atop the deck of the Shipwreck pondering the universe's mysteries may better serve her studies in the long run. Like the armless grandfather clock tocking away in Duane's cave, I can only tell you what is happening now. Everything else is just possibility.

Hello,

Now that you've come to the end of the book, it seems like a good time to give a proper greeting, which I am doing now (with the help of C.C., who is actually writing this letter).

  I was about to introduce myself earlier, just before chapter six, but Major Puff cautioned against it. He thought that we should study you for a while. Magic insisted it would be more fun to surprise you by all of us yelling "Boo!" as soon as you finished the last story. Boo requested that she be left out of it. Both Handsome and Twitch reassured me that I would know in my heart when the proper time was to make your acquaintance. That time, it seems, is now.

You see, I worry that after you put down the book, you'll forget about us. That would be terribly unfortunate, as we were just getting to know each other. I was wondering if we had things in common. For example, do you have a close friend who is a musk ox? What is your personal opinion on bear hugs? I am in favor of them. C.C., who is still writing this, and now shaking her head, is not. What kind of icicles do you have where you live? I don't mean to be nosy. I just think that questions are important when building a friendship.

Before you go, before you close this book, I would like to make a suggestion. Should you find the opportunity to come up north one day, please stop by to say hello in person. We could go exploring together. You could tell me your name. But if you don't have a name, don't worry. I can give you one. C.C. says I'm good at that!

Until then,

DUANE THE POLAR BEAR

Duane's adventures continue in

Just Beyond the Very, Very Far North

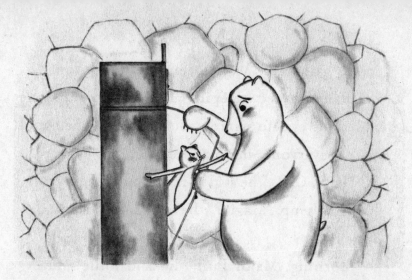

DUANE AWAKES, FINDS HIMSELF AMONG FRIENDS, AND THEN FINDS SOMEONE LESS FRIENDLY

ONE DELIGHTFULLY BITTER, COLD morning, Duane woke up from a long, long, *very* long nap. He stretched what needed stretching. He scratched what needed scratching. He yawned for a full minute and a half. With the claws of his front paw, he brushed his white polar bear fur until he felt that he looked presentable. Then he ventured out of his cave.

"Hello, Duane," said the half dozen individuals

already gathered. "We've been waiting for you."

Duane smiled sleepily. The bright sunshine caused his eyes to narrow, but even still, he could see that everyone who mattered to him was there.

"Hello, C.C.," he said to his friend, a snowy owl.

"What's up, Magic?" he asked his friend, an arctic fox.

"Morning, Major Puff," he said while saluting his friend, a puffin.

"Lovely to see you, Twitch," he said to his friend, an arctic hare.

"Salutations, Handsome," he said to his friend, a musk ox.

"Hi, Boo," he whispered to his skittish friend, a caribou.

Certain that no one had been left out, Duane opened his big, powerful arms as wide as they could spread. "Group hug, everyone!" he declared. And then he pulled all his friends in close, except for C.C., who flew up in the air because, as she's always maintained, she is *not* a touchy-feely kind of owl.

"So what did I miss?" Duane asked.

"What did you miss?" said Magic incredulously. "What did you *miss*? What *didn't* you miss, would be the easier question, Duane." Magic has a tendency to overexcite. The others shuffled their feet or groomed themselves absentmindedly until her point was made and conversation could continue. "You've slept through most of the winter. There have been blizzards and iceberg breakings and strange creature sightings and at least a billion other things. I mean, *really*!"

Duane nodded apologetically, which is Magic's favorite response. Then he said, "In that case, let's begin with what I didn't miss, since the list would surely be smaller."

"You didn't miss the comet, which, according to my calculations, will be flying above us in two weeks. Two weeks!" squealed C.C. with a shudder of delight before gaining control of herself.

"Fortunately for you, you haven't missed my gripping solo reenactment of the Great Puffin War of Eighteen-Something-Or-Other," declared Major Puff proudly. "Will there be marching, you ask? Oh, yes, there will be plenty of marching!" At which Major Puff proceeded to demonstrate by marching around the group with feet raised high.

"And you didn't miss my upcoming birthday, thank goodness," said Handsome, "because etiquette would then require that I give you cold harsh glares of disappointment. Such expressions never look good on me, and all that face-tightening just adds wrinkles."

"You didn't miss my first attempt at public singing," whispered Boo.

"What was that?" asked Duane, but Boo just shook her head self-consciously and hid behind Handsome.

Before any plans for the day could be suggested by his friends, a breeze carried the sweet smell of wild berries up to Duane's nose, which he inhaled to his great delight. His stomach, now stirred and fully awake, wasted no time in growling a plan of action that Duane obediently relayed to the others. "I think a post-nap snack is what's necessary. We could all visit the berry bushes on the way to the Fabulous Beach for a picnic."

Duane's friends know there is no point in arguing with Duane's stomach, and there are worse things to do than spend a day at the beach in one another's company. With little fuss, they made their way down the hillside toward the ocean's edge.

"Might we stop briefly at my abode so I can take

along my brush?" asked Handsome. "I find the salt air tangles my hair, leaving it a matted mess."

"Ooh, and if we pop by me and the Major's place," said Twitch, "I'll bring along some meringue cookies I whipped up this morning. And some carrot cake and a selection of tarts."

"Then that's what we shall do," agreed Duane.

"But Duane," moaned Magic, while flopping on the ground and sighing very dramatically, "then we will never get there!"

"We will. I'm absolutely sure of it." He gave Magic a smile for encouragement. "Major Puff, would you do us the honor?"

"Understood," said the puffin, who rushed toward the front of the group. "Follow me, lads! Left, right, left, right, and so on!"

Duane lingered back, allowing everyone to proceed before him. He took a moment to acknowledge his fortunate circumstances. To think that he'd come to the Very, Very Far North from somewhere else and was able to make himself a home that was cozy, and friends who meant the world to him. Duane sighed, and without a doubt, it was a happy sigh. The day was proving itself to be a very pleasant one, requiring little effort on Duane's part to keep it so. In a short while, he would be eating sweet nibbles and warming his belly under a springtime sun.

But just as he was about to join his friends, a most disagreeable rush of noise overwhelmed him. Clanging and booming and bonging and rumbling, the cacophony was so loud and violent, it shook the ground beneath his paws.

Oh my, thought Duane.

Was it an earthquake? An avalanche? These were questions best left for a less chaotic interlude. At that moment, Duane could only manage to reach up and cover his ears as the din continued to assault him from all sides. He wanted to run away and find safety, but he couldn't. His legs were wobbly, unresponsive; they wouldn't move forward no matter how much he willed them to. Duane was terrified.

Meanwhile, his friends *were* moving farther

and farther away. Soon they would be gone, out of sight and out of hearing range. Oddly enough, they seemed unaffected by the deafening noise. Could they not hear it? Why was it not throwing them off-balance like it was doing to him? These, too, were questions best left for later. Right now, Duane needed their help. He yelled for them to come back, or at least he tried to, because while his legs might have been unsteady, his voice was just plain stuck. It made no sense. His jaw was wide open, his intentions were urgent, yet nothing came out of his mouth but a silent scream.

Now, before you get too swept up in the unsettling, even scary situation I've just described, I will take this moment to tell you that nothing in this story so far is real. Duane hadn't really greeted his friends or planned a picnic or suddenly found himself helplessly in the grasp of an overpowering ruckus. That is because Duane was still in his cozy cave, lying on his soft mattress, having a terrible, terrible nightmare. I apologize.

I should have been more forthcoming about this fact. It's just that in my opinion, no story is ever improved by telling a reader that it has all been a dream. Yet in this case, it's unavoidable. Duane was asleep, albeit fitfully, and even if his nightmare scream was soundless, his real scream—the one that finally woke him up—was very, very loud, as you will soon learn.

"AH!"

Duane sat up in an instant. His face was flushed, and his body was trembling. Those of you who have had bad dreams may recognize Duane's confusion as he took in his surroundings, found his bearings, and realized that he was no longer in the dream but back in his cave, alone.

"Oh my," he whispered aloud.

But although he was awake, the noise had not ceased.

Bong! Clang! Clang! Bong! Clang!

The source of Duane's nightmare was apparently coming from the grandfather clock tucked in the corner. *How unexpected*, thought Duane. For as long as he had had the old timepiece, it had offered nothing in the way of conversation but a steady, calm, and reasonably quiet *tick-tock*. Now, for some unexplained reason, it had decided to add pealing and tolling to the mix, and was doing such, I should add, with reckless abandon.

Clang! Dong! Bong! Bong!

This was most strange. The grandfather clock no longer had hands on its face to tell general time, and therefore had forgone its duty to announce any specific time. Since relocating the clock from the Shipwreck many, many months ago, Duane felt he had come to understand the language of *tick-talking*, so from his point of view, the clock must surely be upset about something important and needed to make it abundantly clear.

"There, there," Duane said to it gently as he walked over. "What seems to be the problem?"

To his surprise, and to yours, too, I should imagine, the grandfather clock spoke back. Amid all the clangs and bongs, an angry voice from within yelled, "Where is it?"

Duane took this in stride. He figured that if he was able to understand clock language, it stood to reason that given enough time, the clock would learn to speak his. "Where is what?" Duane asked.

Bong! Clang! Clang! "Argh! Come on, where did it go?"

Duane leaned in closer. "Perhaps if you describe what you're looking for, I can help you."

"Arrrgh!" growled the clock, seemingly ignoring Duane's generous offer.

But *was* it the clock speaking? Now that Duane was closer, he could hear other sounds besides the clanging and the yelling. He could hear scurrying and scraping as well. Intrigued, Duane used his claws to pry open the long, thin panel on the clock's belly. What he saw inside the grandfather clock, among the weights and chains, the pendulum and other metal doodads noisily flying about, was a small, furry creature who appeared to be in the middle of a big, furious tantrum.